Patient 17L was missing

from the space satellite clinic that orbited the Earth constantly. It was impossible for anyone to simply vanish from such a place, for it was a worldlet of its own, the absolute preserve of its head physician, and no shuttle or lander could hope to approach it in secret and abduct a patient. Yet the man had vanished.

Not just anyone could be treated at such an orbital hospital. Only someone of the maximum importance could gain entry. Only someone with the okay of the top authorities could authorize a bed or a release. This patient was clearly of such a caliber that even the attendants did not know his name or the nature of his medical problem.

But his disappearance had to be reported —to the Earth, to Mars, to the satellites of Jupiter. **And when it was—the Solar System might never be the same again.**

Jeff Sutton is an editorial consultant in the aerospace field and a writer. He is an ex-newspaperman and an ex-marine who was a successful writer of non-fiction until 1959 when he turned to fiction and sold his first novel—a science fiction paperback. Since then he has written and published over a dozen science fiction books in hard covers and paperbound, including *Apollo at Go, Alton's Unguessable, First on the Moon*, and a mainstream novel of the areospace industry, *The Missile Lords*, published by Putnam's.

Mr. Sutton and his family live in La Mesa, California.

THE MINDBLOCKED MAN

JEFF SUTTON

DAW BOOKS, INC.

DONALD A. WOLLHEIM, PUBLISHER

1301 Avenue of the Americas
New York, N. Y.   10019

PRINTED IN U.S.A.

ONE

"Aaaugh!"

He awoke, trembling, the strangled cry on his lips.

The fish eye! The distorted sky! The blob that ate the stars! He convulsed violently as the nightmarish visions fled from the forefront of his mind back into its hidden corners, leaving only the horror of their passage. Shaken, he felt suddenly cold and empty.

As his thoughts cleared, he became aware that he was sprawled face-down on a frayed rug. Alarmed, he pushed himself to a sitting position and looked around. A sagging couch, a table that held a vase of artificial flowers, odds and ends of worn furniture—a strange, nondescript room, yet it held a haunting familiarity that prickled at his memory.

Where am I? Suppressing his uneasiness, he scrutinized his surroundings more critically. A shaft of yellow light filtered through a window adorned with frilly blue drapes that appeared in curious contrast to the room's general drabness. Several doors led to . . . *where?* He stumbled giddily to his feet.

Where am I? The question came again, then, more urgently: *Who am I?* Frantically groping at his memory, he found none beyond the fleeting nightmares which had awakened him. *The distorted sky*—he shivered at the recollection.

Lord, his aching head! He rubbed his temples with tremulous fingertips, his gaze fixed on his thin, pajama-clad body—the bare, bony feet. Extending a hand, he was repelled by the blue veins that ridged its back, the hawkish curve of the all but fleshless fingers.

My God, who am I? The question screamed in his mind. He edged toward the nearest door. Partially open, it disclosed a bathroom. Bracing himself for he knew not

5

what, he entered it and looked into a mirror above the washbasin.

"No!" he exclaimed. He recoiled a step, then regained his courage and looked again into the glass. Thin, pinched, with deep lines etched into the corners of the faded blue eyes, the face confronting him was that of a stranger.

He forced himself to look at the narrow-bridged nose, the tight mouth pulled down at the corners, the thinning brown hair that held the unnatural gloss of dye. The skin was pigmented, weathered with age. A narrow white scar crossed the temple near the hairline, running back around the perimeter of his head. But it was the face itself that appalled him; he looked to be well over seventy years old.

"My God," he whispered. He touched the scar gingerly, felt a tingling sensation. Hastily pulling off his pajama top, he gaped in horror at his wasted body. Jutted outward with dark hollows between, the ribs appeared like sun-bleached bones. Shuddering, he slowly donned the garment and returned to the other room.

Who am I? The question brought a nameless fear. At the same time the room's haunting familiarity perplexed him—it held the echo of something long forgotten.

He went to the window and parted the drapes to peer out onto a narrow street lined with sleazy shops. Weather-scarred balconies above them, a few displaying artificial flowers and plants, identified the section as a residential area for the poorer working classes. How did he know that? He frowned perplexedly.

Several aircars buzzed around a slender gray tower in the distance. Beyond it, a large space freighter rose silently on anti-gravs. The tower marked a space terminal. Space terminal! He groped wildly at the single clue. For a single instant he had the eerie impression that his mind was about to open, that the knowledge he sought would tumble forth; but then the prickling of memory faded, as if a hand had reached into his mind to erase it clean.

He heard a noise at the door and whirled as a young woman came in. She saw him at the same instant and halted, a look of fright on her face. "What are you doing here?" she demanded.

"I . . . don't know." He looked numbly at her. Young, in the middle twenties, he guessed, she had dark hair, a

6

rather plain face. Her cheap skirt and blouse marked her as a worker.

"Don't know?" She moistened her lips nervously.

"I just woke up, found myself here."

"In my front room?"

He nodded, unable to speak.

"Are you sick?" she demanded.

"I . . . don't know."

"Did someone dump you here?"

"I don't know," he repeated numbly. "I just woke up."

"Who are you?" Gathering her courage, she moved a step closer.

"I don't know."

"Don't know?"

"I can't remember." His eyes beseeched her. "Where am I?"

"In my apartment," she answered firmly.

"But . . . where?"

"If you mean the address, it's Three-two-five point four Glade Avenue. Apartment Two-twelve," she added.

"The city?" he mumbled.

"You don't even remember that?" she asked incredulously. "You're in Los Angeles."

"The Capital?"

"You remember that much."

"Not really," he admitted. "It just came to me."

"You are sick," she asserted. "Where are your clothes?"

He smiled ruefully. "I guess I haven't any."

"They dumped you like that?" Her face grew sympathetic. "If you're broke, why didn't they take you to a public ward?"

"I don't know." He fought the desire to weep. "I won't bother you. I'll go away."

"Like that?" she asked incredulously.

He looked down at his pajamas. "They're all I have."

"Wait, I'll get you something." She hurried from the room. Probably going to call the police, he reflected. He went back into the bathroom to peer into the mirror.

Who am I? He stroked his whiskered face wonderingly. Odd, but he knew the names of the objects around him; he could speak, think, recognize his predicament, remember everything clearly from the moment he had awakened. But beyond that, nothing. Except the fish eye. He'd

7

had that wild dream of distorted universes before—of harsh stars blotted out by a huge whirling blob. When? He couldn't remember; the past was a void that defied analysis.

Amnesia? Of course, it had to be. But how had he gotten into the girl's apartment? *Someone had dumped him;* that was her belief. But who? And why here?

He heard her returning and went into the other room to meet her. She was carrying a sleeveless tan shirt and a pair of dark knee-length trousers of the kind commonly worn by manual laborers.

"I got them from a fellow down the hall," she explained. "They're old but it's the best I could do."

"They'll do fine," he answered eagerly.

"Oh, I forgot shoes. What size do you wear?"

"I don't know." He gazed at his bony feet with their ridging blue veins.

"About medium," she guessed. "I'll see what I can find."

"You're very kind."

"I just want to get you out of here."

"I'm sorry to trouble you," he apologized.

"You're not labor, are you?" She stepped closer. "You have a bit of an accent."

"Accent?"

"I can't place it. Were you an outworlder?"

"I don't know." He smiled wistfully. "I wish I did, but I don't."

"Loss of memory happens quite often to old people, even with the shots," she said. She caught the pain in his eyes and exclaimed, "Oh, I didn't mean that."

"I seem quite old," he replied gently.

"Not that old." She forced a smile, peering closer. "Your face is familiar."

"It is?" he asked hopefully.

"Perhaps you live around here."

"I don't know."

"I know I've seen you before."

"That makes me feel better," he asserted.

"Why?"

"I don't feel quite so alone."

"Your memory will come back." She smiled reassuringly. "I'll see about shoes."

When she left, he stripped off the pajamas and donned the shirt and pants. Far too large, they made him appear even more emaciated than he was. Going to the window, he felt the prickling in his brain as he gazed at the slender tower rising up from the space terminal. When had he seen it before? The attempt to answer was almost a pain. But he had seen it before!

He smiled nostalgically at the fleeting impression of *déjà vu*—the knowledge of having lived through this scene before. Somehow the space tower had evoked a feedback from his memory cells, coupling the present with the past.

Who am I? My God, who am I? Would he ever know? The thought that he might not was terrifying. Outworlder, she had guessed. Mars? Or had she meant one of the satellite planets beyond? If that were true, how had he come here? His head began to ache, bringing a nausea that pervaded his entire body. His legs felt weak and tremulous. Footsteps at the door brought him around. She came in bearing a pair of old sandals.

"They're large," she apologized.

"They'll do fine." He slipped them on his feet and tightened the straps. Straightening, he looked at her. "I don't quite know how to thank you."

"That's all right," she answered tonelessly.

"What's your name?"

"Mura . . . Mura Breen."

"That's a pretty name. Quite unusual."

"It's Martian." Her eyes blazed defiantly.

"You're from Mars?"

"Noachis, near the dead sea Serpentis."

"Noachis, I remember."

"You've been there?" she asked sharply.

"I don't believe so." He shook his head. "It's just the memory of a name. Why did you come to Earth?"

"Please," she begged.

"I'm sorry, I'd better be going." He moved toward the door.

"Where to?"

"I don't know."

"Have you a charge plate? No, of course you haven't. Then how will you live?"

"I'll manage," he replied uncertainly.

"Without a charge plate?" She shook her head. "Why

9

don't you let me call the police? They'll take you to a public clinic."

"No," he exclaimed. He felt a surge of fear.

"Why not? Have you done something wrong?"

"I don't believe so."

"You can't wander the streets like that," she remonstrated.

"I have to find out who I am," he explained.

"The police will do that for you."

"No, I have to find out for myself." He walked out into a dingy hall, spotted the stairwell, and started toward it.

"Wait," she called. Even the few steps had drained him. She eyed him worriedly. "If you can't find a place, come back. You can sleep on the couch."

"I'll be all right." He turned and slowly descended the stairs. When he stepped outside and gazed around, he again felt a haunting sense of familiarity. *Who am I?*

Straightening his thin shoulders, he started along the street.

17L was missing!

The white-gowned attendant stared stupidly at the empty hospital bed. How could a drugged patient be missing? His eyes, darting wildly around the small cubicle, told him that the impossible was possible. He hurriedly examined the remaining half a dozen cubicles; all were empty. So was surgery. He dashed into the galley. The cook looked up, startled.

"Have you seen the patient?"

"The patient? My God, is he ... "

"Have you seen him?" the attendant shouted.

"No."

"Has anyone gone down into maintenance?"

"N-no one," the cook stuttered. The attendant ran back into the corridor and pounded on the nurse's door.

"What is it?" she called.

"Seventeen-L is missing," he hissed softly.

"Missing?" She pulled the door open, her face ashen. "Impossible!"

"But he is," he blurted.

"Have you tried the galley?"

10

"The galley, maintenance—he's nowhere!" he exclaimed.

"The landers?"

"The landers, of course!" He snapped his fingers and started toward the outboard wells. Both landers were there, both empty. He swung back, licking his lips nervously.

"He might be with Dr. Sundberg," she suggested nervously.

"How could he be? He's drugged to the ears."

"Go see," she urged.

"It's no use." Nevertheless he went to a door at the end of the corridor and pressed a button. A chime sounded softly on the other side.

"What is it?" a voice called testily.

"Kelsey. I have to see you."

"Come in." Dr. Gerald Sundberg, fortyish, slender, with a high, gleaming forehead, regarded him with annoyance. "Well . . . ?"

Kelsey gulped and said, "Seventeen-L is missing."

"Missing?" Sundberg exclaimed incredulously. He leaped up from his chair. "That is impossible!"

"He's gone!"

"Have you looked in the other recovery rooms, the galley?"

"I've searched the ship, every inch."

"The landers?"

"They're both in their wells, empty."

"It's impossible, I tell you!" Sundberg banged a fist on the desk. "Search again."

"Yes, sir." As the attendant withdrew, Sundberg went to a port and looked out; the Sky Haven Clinic was racing down over the top of the world. Ice fields wheeled past beneath him. Far ahead, to the left, he saw the purple blur of mountains rising from the polar forests.

He looked at his hand—it was shaking—then returned to his desk and slumped down. Escape from the clinic was impossible! No lander could have approached without setting off the detector alarms; kidnapping was out. Neither could he have been spirited from the clinic without inside connivance. Sundberg gazed wanly at his hands; he couldn't remember when last they'd trembled.

"Craxton Wehl"—he croaked the missing man's name

11

softly. Both the nurse and Kelsey knew the patient's true identity, of course. So did the cook and maintenance help; but none ever had acknowledged it. He was simply 17L, a record designation, as were others who sought Sundberg's services from time to time.

But Craxton Wehl's case was different. Vastly different! The mere contemplation of it brought the sweat to his brow. Craxton Wehl, premier, the most powerful figure in the Solar Empire, had ruled as a not-too-gentle despot for more than thirty years. His word had been absolute law.

At age seventy-six, paranoiac and in rapidly failing health, Wehl had come to him for help—had placed his life in Sundberg's hands. Almost as abruptly, he had announced that he would pass the power. Bernard Rayburn, his hand-picked successor, had been a political unknown from the tiny satellite world of Europa, third out of the Jovian moons.

The succession ceremony, held in the satellite clinic, saw Wehl step down, Rayburn step up; in that instant the latter's word had become absolute law. All that was a matter of public record; but what had happened to the old man afterward was not. Ostensibly a patient, he had been held absolute prisoner. Now he had vanished.

And the new premier was dying!

The gods were against him, Sundberg reflected. He cursed the day he'd first taken Wehl as a patient. Since then, machinations within machinations had pinned him to the wall. Now the new premier, shadowed by death, had to return the power. But how could he return it to a man who wasn't there?

How had he gotten into such a predicament? He smiled bitterly. Not that he'd had a choice. He'd bowed to power. Refusing would have been tantamount to cutting his own throat. Still, he hadn't contemplated that the whole affair could blow up in his face. He could wind up practicing medicine on Pluto. The thought was frightening. He wondered again if he should flee.

The chimes sounded. "Come in," he called hopefully. Kelsey entered, his face white under the soft glow of the zen tubes.

"He's gone," he exclaimed hoarsely.

"How long was he alone?" snapped Sundberg. He spoke louder than he should, attempting to override his own fears through the exertion of authority. Kelsey shifted uneasily. He'd been under strict orders never to leave the patient's side except when the nurse was present. "Well?" demanded Sundberg.

"I just stepped out for coffee," he protested.

"For how long?"

"Not more than a minute."

"Put out your hand." Sundberg reached for an electrode, snapped it on the attendant's finger, and asked, "What do you know about Seventeen-L's disappearance?"

"Nothing," Kelsey answered flatly.

Sundberg watched a needle dance on a dial face before it settled down, then yanked off the electrode. "Send in Nurse Caldwell," he snapped.

Ten minutes later, after all the members of his staff had successfully passed the lie detector test, he leaned back and shut his eyes. Good Lord, the man had been a teleport! Could the brain surgery have unleashed some latent talent? Inconceivable as it seemed, he could find no other answer. He swore softly. Less than a score of teleports in the entire system, now 17L was one of them!

"Damn Wehl," he gritted. What could he do? The premier would have his neck. Not officially, perhaps, but unofficially; that sort of thing happened often enough. But could the premier afford revenge? The question stirred his hope. Not if he were dying. Not with Franckel waiting in the wings to seize power! Despite the old man's condition, the premier urgently needed him. He had to produce the missing patient, and quickly. If he didn't, and the premier died . . .

He forced himself to think of the consequences. The empire would be up for grabs. Franckel, Montre, Gullen—all three were hungrily eyeing the Big Power Seat. Of the three, Franckel was strongest. Still, the struggle could tear the empire to shreds.

He slowly folded and unfolded his hands while considering possible courses of action. He could attempt to find his missing patient; he could hide; he could tell the premier the truth—that the man had teleported. Would that story be believed? Scarcely!

Hide. The word came back. Could he hide from Jing Lee Hom? Hom was a bloodhound. *But if he could hide?* In that event, when the premier died, his successor undoubtedly would have but scant interest in investigating the reasons why he'd failed to produce Wehl. More likely that person—Franckel?—would prove extremely grateful.

But he couldn't hide! He knew that with finality. Jing Lee Hom would find him if he had to tear apart every atom in the universe. He'd find him and send him to Pluto. Hiding was out. So then what? He nervously considered it.

Felix Quigg. He let the name unfold in his mind. Quigg was far and away the best private intelligence operator in the business. Unscrupulous, yes, but good. And expensive. Quigg didn't come cheap. *Big Fees Bring Big Results*—that was Quigg's motto. Lord knows he'd seen it on the triscreen often enough. But the man could produce, a rare thing in a world of nonproducers.

If he could get Quigg! The thought that perhaps he couldn't dismayed him. Quigg had the reputation of being extremely selective. Could he appeal to Quigg's patriotism? No, that was out; Quigg didn't concern himself with that kind of foolishness. A big fee—that was the only talking point he had. He had to shake the money tree, shake it hard. Quigg liked to hear the golden apples drop.

He lifted the laser phone and got through to the nurse. "Get me Felix Quigg," he instructed. "If you have any difficulty, tell him it concerns the Big Power Seat." He broke the connection with savage satisfaction. That should bring Quigg running.

The phone tinkled to life in amazingly short time. He pressed a button and watched a small screen flare to life. The raucous sound of Martian nose flutes leaped from the instrument, and the green and orange sign that filled the screen read:

FELIX QUIGG & ASSOCIATES
WE COVER THE EMPIRE
NO JOB UNDER 50,000 CPU

Fifty thousand charge plate units! Sundberg winced, waiting impatiently. When the commercial ended, Felix Quigg's suave, polished face replaced the sign. Sundberg barked, "Quigg, I need you right away."

"Sorry, Sundberg, I'm booked for months three."

"This is a matter of empire security, Quigg."

"There's no security except what you buy."

"I'm shaking the money tree," he exclaimed hoarsely.

"That bad, eh? State the terms."

"Seventy-five thousand cpu."

"Seventy-five thousand charge plate units?" Quigg laughed nastily. "Why did you bother to call?"

"One hundred thousand cpu for successful performance," he shot back.

"I don't like the qualification," Quigg countered.

"One hundred thousand fixed fee plus fifty percent for successful performance, Quigg. That's all I can crop."

"The advance?"

"Fifty thousand to your charge plate. I'll initiate it immediately."

"Who's your guarantor?"

Sundberg hesitated. "Craxton Wehl," he said finally.

"That's not the Big Power Seat, Sundberg. An ex-premier's like an ex-mistress—nothing but a damned nuisance."

Sundberg dropped his voice. "Premier Rayburn is involved."

"As guarantor?"

"Of course." He groped with his thoughts. "But he can't afford to be directly involved. You understand that."

"I'll buy. What performance is required?"

"A missing person. I need him back here in a hurry."

"Name?"

"Craxton Wehl."

TWO

Dark, sharp-featured, with quick-moving black eyes, Felix Quigg was considered by many to be the top private intelligence operator in the empire. Reputedly a man who would do anything for money, many whispered he often had. He listened intently as Sundberg related his troubles.

15

When the medic finished, Quigg asked, "So Wehl vanished, eh?"

"Like that." Sundberg snapped his fingers.

"Connivance."

"I don't believe so."

"We'll get to that." Quigg smiled frostily. "Let's discuss the angles."

"Angles?"

"You hired me to do a job," Quigg snapped. "Don't stall. Why did Wehl come to you as a patient?"

"That's a professional confidence, Quigg."

"I'm waiting."

"He was in failing health," Sundberg said reluctantly. He leaned with his elbows on the desk and formed a steeple with his fingers while wondering how much he could divulge safely. "He was afraid he didn't have long to live."

"Why would he come here to die?"

"The Sky Haven Clinic is the House of Hope, Quigg. That's our motto."

"Don't try to klotch me. Why did he come here?"

"Well, confidentially . . . "

"Come off it, Sundberg."

The medic flushed and said, "He had a nervous breakdown."

"What symptoms? Be specific."

"He was paranoiac, believed everyone was out to assassinate him."

"Small wonder."

"He also realized the precarious condition of his health. That's what prompted him to step down, pass the power to Rayburn."

"That doesn't ring true, Sundberg. I wondered about it at the time."

"Why doesn't it?" he asked defiantly.

"Wehl was power-mad if ever a man was. He could have appointed Rayburn to the Big Power Seat effective at time of his own death. That was the more logical course."

"His daughter persuaded him."

"Madelyn?" Quigg snickered. "She's as power-mad as he is."

"I'm Wehl's physician, remember? He confided in me.

16

Paranoid delusions, Quigg. He feared that if he appointed Rayburn on those terms, Rayburn might hasten the process."

"Did he actually state that?"

"Absolutely. He believed that by passing the power, he could buy time, at least die in peace. He was focusing the heat on Rayburn."

"You're holding out, Sundberg."

"It's the truth," he cried.

"Shaking the money tree to the tune of one hundred thousand plus fifty percent for successful performance to get back a man who's practically dead? There's something you're not telling me."

Sundberg stared indecisively at him. "Rayburn's dying," he finally admitted.

Quigg's head snapped up. "The premier's dying?"

"Europa fever."

"Your story stinks."

"Why?" he demanded.

"Rayburn's big and young and tough. He was splashed on every triscreen in the system when he arrived here from Europa. That's the main thing they played up—his youth, his vigor. Now you're trying to tell me he's dying. You're trying to klotch me, Sundberg."

"It's the truth," he cried hoarsely.

"Then someone's trying to klotch you."

"I'm a medic, Quigg, I know. He's got Europa fever. He showed the first symptoms a few days after taking over the Big Power Seat."

Quigg shook his head. "Too coincidental."

"You're an expert on Europa fever?"

"I'm an expert on coincidences. I wouldn't put my charge plate on that one. It spells *klotch*: K-L-O-T-C-H."

"Wrong." Sundberg struggled to regain his composure. "They brought him here in secrecy and I gave him the works. Not that he didn't already know what he had. That stuff's been killing them off on Europa ever since they colonized that berg. It's Europa fever, all right, and there's no known cure. Rayburn has perhaps two weeks to go, three at most. I'd stake my reputation on that."

"How did he take it?"

"Oh, it shook him, but it didn't shake his thought processes. He realized immediately that he either had to

17

return the empire to Wehl to prevent, ah, one of the governors from seizing power, or to prevail on Wehl to recommend another successor."

"Why didn't he ask Wehl when he came up for the check? Wehl was here; you said so yourself."

"It wasn't that simple."

"Why not?"

"Secret of State, Quigg."

"The lid's off," Quigg snapped. "I need the facts."

"My God, Quigg, that information is classified at the Q level!"

"There's no such thing as secrecy, Sundberg. Secrecy ended the day they invented the whisper. So out with it."

"I'd performed surgery to remove a small tumor from Wehl's brain," Sunberg admitted. "I couldn't get it with sonics; I had to go in with the knife. I feel certain that the tumor was the reason for his delusions. At any rate, the surgery left him with a temporary loss of memory."

"Amnesia?" asked Quigg sharply.

"A temporary condition, I'm positive."

"How temporary?"

"That's difficult to say, but I'm certain I can clear it up with a bit of treatment." Sundberg shifted uneasily. "I can't afford even a whisper of that to get out, Quigg."

"Surgery on an ex-premier? What's so hot about that?"

"If it became known that he wasn't, ah, competent, the knowledge might be used to prevent Rayburn from returning the power to him, or to negate any recommendation Wehl might make. Can't you see what Franckel or one of the other governors might do with a thing like that? It fits under the competency laws," Sundberg declared. "They'd take it to the High Court."

"The High Court," Quigg sneered. "The premier is the High Court, Sundberg, and you know it. Those other jokers are window dressing."

"In normal times, yes, but these aren't normal times, Quigg."

"So if Rayburn dies without passing the power?"

"You know the answer." Sundberg gestured helplessly. "Franckel of Eurasia, Montre of the Americas, Gullen of Mars—they'd tear apart the empire in their battle for power."

"Wehl wouldn't give a damn." Quigg shook his head.

"He's too self-centered to care about what happens after he's gone."

"Wrong!" Sundberg's eyes glinted triumphantly. "You don't understand the ego, Quigg. Wehl's ego is enormous. If you doubt that, ask yourself why a thousand parks bear his name, ten thousand avenues. How many thousands of statues of him has the government manufactured for free distribution to the schools? That's the size of his ego. He'd grab back the power in a second if it were to protect his image in history."

"I doubt it. He's the kind who believes history will end with his passing."

"Our problem is Rayburn," Sundberg said crossly. "He wants him back—wants to return the power. He has a social conscience."

"Those colonists usually have." Quigg studied him. "Where does Madelyn Wehl stand in all this?"

"Well ... "

"What's her stake?"

"None to speak of."

"Cerebrate, Sundberg."

"Well, if Wehl came back into power, her balloon would be up again, of course. But that would last only for as long as it took him to appoint another successor. That's not much of a stake."

"Did she oppose his stepping down?"

"She encouraged it. I told you that."

"Did she approve her father's choice?"

"Of his successor? Loud and clear."

"How does Rayburn feel about her?"

"They jibe, Quigg. Why shouldn't they? Rayburn owes his power to her father."

"That doesn't mean a thing."

"The Congress of Governors gave Madelyn the Wehl House in perpetuity, plus upkeep, maintenance, and a fat yearly retainer," Sundberg explained. "Of course Wehl engineered the deal, but Rayburn went along with it. That certainly reflects his regard."

"It doesn't figure."

"What doesn't?"

"Wehl's selection; that's what I'm getting at. Rayburn was a Mr. Nobody, a dome-dweller from Europa, a hick from Methanville. Something hasn't surfaced, Sundberg. How did Wehl happen to choose him?"

"Politics, I suppose."

"Don't try to klotch me!"

"The selection was designed to keep peace with the OutSats, Quigg. Those dome-dwellers have been pretty damned perturbed over the kind of governors we keep shoving down their throats. Also, it was designed to prevent Franckel, Montre, and Gullen from waging a power battle. By naming Rayburn, he pulled their fangs."

"Did he? The law states the premier has to be Earth-born, Sundberg. Franckel's not convinced that Rayburn meets that requirement. He publicly challenged that point."

"After Rayburn's birth certificate was stolen from the public records," answered Sundberg testily. "His family copy proved that he was born right here in Los Angeles."

"A copy." Quigg sniffed.

"Wehl was satisfied."

"He pushed Rayburn down a lot of throats, Sundberg."

"What has all this to do with finding Wehl?" he snapped.

"I need the facts, the background. I'm still not satisfied with the reasons for Rayburn's selection."

"What's your point?"

"Did Rayburn wield that kind of power? I never heard of him until Wehl uncorked him as the heir."

"He pulled weight out among the gas giants, Quigg."

"Enough to give him the Big Power Seat?" Quigg shook his head. "Something smells, Sundberg. And if the situation is as you say, and Wehl's at the end of the line, what's so important about getting him back? Why can't Rayburn make his own selection?"

"You're not with it," Sundberg shot back irritably. "Wehl's better fitted to make the selection. He knows the power lines, Quigg. Rayburn realizes that. He's held power less than two weeks. Would you expect him to pass on a decision that big? He needs Wehl and needs him badly. The empire needs him, Quigg."

"Another good samaritan concerned with the common cause, eh?"

"They're not all bastards, Quigg."

"Most are. If the situation is as you say, why doesn't he

take his guidance from Madelyn? She certainly knows the power structure."

Sundberg said uncomfortably, "I understand he's acting on her advice. I've given it to you straight, Quigg."

"All but one thing."

"What's that?" asked Sundberg guardedly.

"How did Wehl escape from this trap. Don't tell me he was kidnaped."

"He teleported."

"Sundberg!"

"So help me, it's the truth."

"Wehl a teleport? Never!" Quigg shook his head. "There's not a score of those birds in the system, Sundberg. What are you trying to cover? Did he die in surgery?"

"Certainly not," he snapped indignantly.

"People have been buried in space before, Sundberg."

"Not my patients. I'm a psychosurgeon, Quigg, not a butcher."

"Then how did he get away?"

"I told you, he teleported."

Quigg smiled nastily. "After seventy-some years he turns out to be a teleport, is that what you're trying to tell me?"

"The surgery caused it," Sundberg returned hotly. "The talent must have been latent—was freed when I went into the cortex. Perhaps new neural pathways were formed."

"How far can a teleport jump?" Quigg demanded. "The record is somewhat under five miles. Your perigee here is nearly two hundred. How do you explain that?"

"Do we really know that?" demanded Sundberg. "Who gives out the records? The teleports! How do we know what those birds really can do? The Jumpers League is a damned furtive bunch, Quigg. One theory has it that a man can jump into infinity."

"Infinity," Quigg sneered.

"I wouldn't bank that one couldn't."

"You've been connived."

"Then you tell me how he got away."

"Have you put your staff through the wringer? I'll warrant that you'll find one of them with an overly fat charge plate."

"I checked them, Quigg. They're clean."

"A teleport," Quigg grated, "and you pushed the job off on me for a lousy one hundred thousand."

"With a fifty percent bonus for successful completion," the doctor quickly reminded. He added smugly, "I recorded our call and posted fifty thousand cpu's to your charge plate. That legalizes the contract."

"We'll have to renegotiate."

"The contract stands!"

"You hid a vital factor," Quigg returned. "I can tear up the contract and laugh in your face and you know it. It's a pure klotch."

"What factor?"

"The teleport angle. If Wehl spots me he'll leap all over the planet. I'll have to hire a peeper to read his destination, then perhaps we can get him with a sleep dart."

"No peeper!" Sundberg shouted with alarm. He felt positively ill at what a peeper might discover.

"Why not?"

"Rayburn would have my throat. Yours, too."

"He wants Wehl back, doesn't he?"

"No peeper, Quigg." Sundberg pulled himself together. "State secrets, you know. A premier's mind is sacrosanct, and that applies to ex-premiers. Peep Wehl and you'd wind up in a cave out on Pluto. You couldn't make that part of the contract stick." Sundberg shivered at the thought.

"It's a pure klotch, Sundberg."

"Not if you return Wehl."

"Oh, I'll return him. I never fail."

"Then what's your worry?"

"Your story," Quigg snapped. "It stinks. Who do you have aboard?"

"The nurse, an attendant, the cook, and one maintenance." Sundberg ticked them off on his fingers.

"Do they subscribe to your weird theory?"

"The teleport angle? I thought it best not to mention that. They don't know what happened."

"I'll interview them," Quigg decided.

"Now?" Sundberg reached for a button.

Quigg stopped him. "Privately, one at a time," he advised. "I don't want them cooking up something among themselves."

"They're trustworthy. I can vouch for every one of them."

"When someone shakes the money tree?"

"Well ... "

"The fat conscience knows no remorse, Sundberg. The corollary of that is that you have to fatten the conscience to live with it, and money's the food. Personally, my own trust stops with my charge plate."

"I'm not that cynical, Quigg."

"Come into the real world, Sundberg." Quigg leaned toward him. "There's one other thing."

"What?" Sundberg waited.

"I'd like to put you through the wringer. Clip on the electrode."

"Never!" Sundberg recoiled violently. "It's against the medical code, Quigg. Doctors are the keepers of too many confidences. You'll have to take me at my word."

"If you try to klotch me ... "

"Why should I? It's my neck if you don't find Wehl."

"Does the premier know he's missing?"

"Not yet." Sundberg shifted uneasily.

Quigg leaned back and relaxed. "I saw your nurse on the way in. She's a real sizzler."

"She's quite professional," Sundberg rebutted stiffly.

"What's her name?"

"Nurse Caldwell."

"I'll speak to her first," Quigg decided.

"Shall I have her come in?"

"I'll go to her quarters." Quigg smirked. "Privacy, you know."

Sundberg was trying to klotch him!

Quigg felt certain of that as he prepared to depart from the clinic. The entire story held an improbable ring. Wehl's voluntary passing of the power had strained his credulity at the time. That Madelyn had urged the move was equally incredible. Now, after two short weeks, Rayburn was dying.

He grimaced frostily. To top it off, Wehl had amnesia, was missing, and—after more than thirty years of public exposure as premier—had proved to be a teleport. What was the statistical probability of that chain of events?

23

But Sundberg's staff was clean. He had satisfied himself in that respect. The thought brought a frown. Nurse Caldwell had proved quite uncooperative in the matter of what he might be able to do for her. Clearly Sundberg had her in his corner. And Kelsey? Kelsey was dumb.

"I'll be in touch," he told Sundberg at the lander well.

"You'll have to work fast," the medic urged worriedly.

"We never fail, Sundberg. Don't you follow our ads?" Before the other could reply, he stepped into the lander and closed the door. Programming his reentry on the autopilot, he punched a button, felt a slight lurch as the lander slid free. A swath of starry sky sprang into view on a screen above the console.

As the lander went into brief retrofire and began dropping, he settled back to contemplate the possibilities. Wehl *could* have passed the power to Rayburn legitimately enough; Rayburn *could* be dying; Wehl *could* have teleported—that was one set of possibilities.

Could Wehl have been tricked out of the power— drugged, his responses programmed? Could Sundberg, working for Franckel or one of the other governors, have disposed of Wehl when it became known that Rayburn was dying? That would pave the way nicely for a power grab. Or could Sundberg simply have botched the job, disposed of Wehl to protect his reputation? In that event hiring him was part of the cover-up.

Quigg frowned. That latter possibility meant a barren money tree—nothing beyond the one hundred thousand fixed fee. He'd have to take a positive approach. Alive, Wehl was fuel to the charge plate, especially with the stakes as they were. If Sundberg could shake the money tree for one hundred thousand cpu's plus a fifty percent bonus for successful completion, how much might someone else go?

Franckel, Montre, Gullen, Madelyn Wehl—he ticked off the names in his mind. If Franckel or one of the other governors bought, it would be for the purpose of disposing of Wehl; that would clear the way for the seizure of power when Rayburn died. Franckel was strongest, he mused. If Franckel bought, he'd have to dispose of Montre and Gullen, but those things could be arranged. The same applied if he sold to either Montre or Gullen.

Madelyn Wehl was a quite different matter. Her public

24

image was a vain and selfish woman, a fit daughter for the old man. Quigg couldn't beleive that bit about her urging her father to step down. That wasn't in her character. But Wehl's restoration would send her own balloon soaring again, if even for a short while. Yes, she'd shake the money tree—shake it hard.

A deal with her would be the safest course, he reflected. Franckel or any other potential buyer might feel compelled to have him assassinated afterward to shut his mouth; but Madelyn should feel quite grateful.

That was one thing.

But what was the real story? Sundberg's explanation had been all gloss. He hadn't missed the man's fright at the suggestion of hiring a peeper. Perhaps the secret, if he knew it, could double or triple Wehl's value.

Could he risk having Wehl's mind probed? Not by a peeper, certainly. The few who might be available undoubtedly had ties with the police—more probably with Empire Intelligence. Jing Lee Hom wasn't one to allow a peeper to roam without some kind of a wire on him. But there were other ways—narcohypnosis, for one. And if Wehl had amnesia, he'd remember nothing about it later on.

He contemplated the possibilities. If anyone knew what the real stakes were, that person would be Craxton Wehl. The best-known face in the Solar Empire, Quigg reflected. Locating him should be easy. He punched a button on the laser phone, barked a coded number, and waited impatiently through the commercial until his secretary's face filled the small screen.

"Have Arthur check the police precincts for an amnesia pickup," he instructed crisply. He gave the details, terminated the call, and settled back.

He could fairly hear the wind in the money tree.

THREE

He walked slowly, his body aching with a fatigue that seemed to permeate its every cell. His head throbbed and his eyes, slightly out of focus, brought a nausea that made him ill all over.

Despite his discomfort, he interestedly eyed the sleazy shops, the jostling passersby, and the aircars that flitted like birds above the rooftops. There was no vehicular surface traffic, of course; none was allowed in the heart of the city. But he could sense it rumbling underfoot through the traffic tubes.

How did he know the tubes were there? How did he know all of the things he knew yet didn't know, at least at the memory level? Was he a creature of pure stimulus-response, capable of reaction only to his immediate environment? No, he could think, reason—at least back to the instant when he had awakened. But beyond that a gray veil enveloped his mind. Except for the fish eye! The fish eye and the distorted sky!

God, who am I? The agonizing question seared his mind. Threading his way among the pedestrians, he studied the ebb and flow of life—a mosaic of faces that all seemed to blend into one. A gigantic, bizarre, alien face, its dimensions were characterless. Yet, from time to time, as when he gazed at the slender tower of the space terminal, he felt the quick prickling of recognition. Even this very street, and Mura's apartment, brought fleeting shadows of memory that faded almost before they were formed.

It was, he reflected, like passing through a Stygian cave, aided only by the flickering light of a candle. His glimpses of the past were like that—flickering and illusory. How could he seize on such an instant, retain it, analyze it? Perhaps if he solved one mystery he could solve them all. The hope burned fiercely.

26

Thought of Mura Breen brought a warmth. At first she had seemed quite plain; later, her face had radiated a warmth that had made her quite beautiful. Now if he were forty years younger ... The contemplation quickened his pulses.

He came to a small park and sat on one of the benches to watch the mechanical pigeons. Restricted to an island formed by a small moat, they hopped back and forth, pecking at artificial grain. Once, centuries before, such birds had existed, but had been exterminated as carriers of disease. The resulting outcry from the seniors who liked to bask in the parks had caused the government to recreate the birds in mechanical form. Now such pigeons—Model 23H—were to be found in the parks of every large city.

How had he known that? The question puzzled him. But he knew it; and to know it, he'd had to reach back into the unreachable. Did that mean that his memory was surfacing? Lord, his name, his name. *Who am I? Who? Who? Who?* Sighing, he leaned back and closed his eyes, feeling the sun's warmth on his face. After a while he dozed.

"You there, wake up!"

He struggled to consciousness and saw the tan-clad figure of a policeman looming over him. "I must have dozed," he mumbled.

"Sleeping in a public park violates code two-four-three-five," the officer rasped.

"I'm sorry."

"What's your name?"

"Name?" He groped frantically with his thoughts, then blurted, "Gerald Sundberg." As the name escaped his lips, he wondered from what depths he'd drawn it. A name! He felt a sweep of elation. *He was ... He was Gerald Sundberg!*

"Gerald Sundberg, eh? Where's your I.D.?"

"Identification?" He fumbled in his pocket while trying to think of an excuse. "I must have forgotten it," he muttered.

"The law requires that you have it with you at all times. That violates code one-seven-eight-one. Do you have a charge plate?"

He sat straighter. "Does the code require one?"

"As a means of identification."

27

"Yes, certainly." He fumbled in his pocket again. "I must have left it at home."

"Where do you live?"

"Down there." He gestured in the direction from which he had come.

"Be specific," the officer snapped.

"Yes, of course." He remembered Mura's address but pushed it resolutely from his mind; he couldn't risk involving her.

"Well?"

He grasped at the first number that came to mind and said, "I live at Four-twelve Glade Avenue."

The officer lifted an arm, snapped a button on a wrist radio, and barked, "Hansen to I.D. computer. Give me the names of the occupants at Four-twelve Glade." He waited, listened to the tinkling reply, then snapped off the set and said accusingly, "You don't live there."

"I . . . must have forgotten."

"Giving false information to a police officer violates"— the policeman drew a small indexed book from his pocket and checked it—"code one-three-two-six."

"My memory slips at times," he protested.

"That happens with old ones." The officer snapped on the wrist radio and said, "Hansen to Patrol Seven; I'm holding a vag at Craxton Wehl Park."

"I'm no vag," he pleaded.

"Tell it to the desk sergeant."

He started to argue, then realized the futility of it and desisted. Waiting, he wondered what kind of a world it was that would penalize an old man for basking in the sun. If they didn't want people to rest in the park, why the mechanical pigeons? Sensing that it might violate some code or other, he refrained from asking.

A shadow splashed across the square and he looked up, seeing an aircar approaching. The crossed blasters on the nose identified it as one of the urban peace patrols. A light humming reached his ears as the vehicle settled to the pavement alongside them. The officer opened the rear door and snapped, "Inside."

He entered wearily, sitting behind a metal grate that separated him from the driver. His companion stuck his head into the front compartment. "Tapes on, Frank?"

"Tapes on," the driver assented.

28

The officer cited the code violations. "He claims his name is Gerald Sundberg but I can't verify it," he finished.

"Gerald Sundberg?" The driver wrinkled his face. "Isn't that the name of that medic who runs the orbital clinic? Sure it is, the House of Hope; I've seen the ad a thousand times. It won some kind of a prize as the best mercy message of the year."

"This stiff's no medic, Frank."

"The name's the same; I'm certain of that."

The arresting officer consulted his index again. "If you find he's given me a phony, add four-one-one-six to the violations."

"Check, anything else?"

"Yeah, I'll trade you jobs. This pavement kills my feet."

"You should try sitting all day." The driver grinned, closed the front window, and lifted the aircar into the traffic flow.

Gerald Sundberg: could that possibly be his name? It had to be, he thought fiercely. *Sundberg, Sundberg, Sundberg—he was Gerald Sundberg.* He let the miracle of the name unfold in his mind. Now he was somebody; he was Gerald Sundberg! He had identity.

But was he Gerald Sundberg? He fought unsuccessfully to reject the disquieting question. If the name wasn't his, why had it come so readily to mind? Watching the buildings slip past beneath him, he pondered it. There was another Gerald Sundberg; the driver had been quite positive. A medic. Could there be two Gerald Sundbergs? Perhaps. "I am Gerald Sundberg," he told himself. That was his name; he'd answer to no other. He felt a touch of pride and sat straighter.

The aircar broke from the traffic pattern, circled, and descended toward a landing platform atop a rather dilapidated building. When it touched down, the driver leaped out and opened the rear door. "Out, Mr. Sundberg," he ordered.

"Thank you." He nodded appreciatively at the recognition of his name as he stepped out. It had a certain ring that he liked. He accompanied his escort to an elevator that creaked its way to the ground floor. When the door opened, he was taken to the desk sergeant.

"Present from Hansen," the patrol officer said.

"Name?"

"Gerald Sundberg."

"Charge?"

His escort recited the violations. "If the name's a phony, you can add four-one-one-six," he added.

"Where was he apprehended?"

"Craxton Wehl Park."

The desk sergeant switched his gaze. "Is that your right name?"

"Yes, Gerald Sundberg."

"Good enough. I'll knock off the four-one-one-six, cut down on the paper work." The sergeant's fingers played over an adding machine. Glancing at the results, he said, "Bail comes to three hundred and ten cpu's."

"He has no charge plate," the patrol officer said.

"No charge plate?" The sergeant eyed the prisoner bleakly. "That's tank talk, Sundberg."

"I must have left it somewhere," he explained.

"So you can't pay your bail, eh?"

"Well . . . "

"No charge plate, no I.D. card, giving false information to a police officer, and sleeping in the park. That's quite a record, Sundberg. How do you explain it?"

"Sleeping in the park?"

"All of it."

"I don't know. My memory's not what it used to be." He looked up quizzically. "Or is that another violation?"

"Very funny," the sergeant snapped. He leaned across the desk. "I'm beginning to doubt very much that you are Gerald Sundberg. For being smart, I'm going to make you prove it. Until you do, I'm slapping you with a four-one-one-six. What do you think of that?"

"Not much," he admitted.

"Throw him in the tank," the sergeant snarled.

"This way." His escort grabbed his arm and steered him out into the corridor. Turned over to a jailer, he was led to a cell block. When the steel door clanged shut and he was left alone, he sank down on the narrow cot and buried his face in his hands.

"I am Gerald Sundberg," he told himself desperately. They couldn't take away his name; they couldn't do that. A man had to be somebody and he was somebody; he was Gerald Sundberg. *I am, I am, I am.*

After a while he went to the small barred window and peered out. The sun, sliding down in the west, splashed the nearby buildings with a golden light. The sight stirred his memory, but in such a nebulous way he couldn't be certain it was memory at all. The past, the present, the future—they all dwelt together in the human mind. Returning to the cot, he sat down and massaged his aching calves.

He had to admit that it had been quite a day.

The premier's secretary sympathetically eyed the tall, yellow-haired figure sitting behind the massive desk. His tawny eyes and lean face held the fatigued look of a man who had gone too many hours without sleep. But it wasn't that, she knew. *Bernard Rayburn was doomed!* The whisper had been sweeping the administrative center. Seeing him now, his pallor and tiredness, she well could believe it. And she was sorry.

"Colonel Jing Lee Hom," she announced in a subdued voice.

"Show him in." Watching her withdraw, he smiled faintly. *She knew. Everyone knew.* But that was all to the good; the empire would be prepared. A moment later she returned, standing aside to admit the slender, olive-faced agent who headed the Empire Intelligence cadre assigned to the premier's personal protection.

"Good morning, Colonel." Rayburn gestured him to sit down.

"Good morning, Mr. Premier." Hom nodded politely.

"I'll try to be brief," he said. "Were you aware that following the succession ceremony Wehl underwent surgery for a brain tumor?"

"Not the specifics," Hom admitted. "I realized he was having difficulties."

"The tumor was the reason for his previous mental disturbances," the premier confided. "I'm happy to say that the operation was a complete success. Craxton Wehl should enjoy a number of years of good life."

"I'm happy to hear that." Hom's eyes were questioning.

"That brings us to our present problem."

The agent waited.

"I am dying, Colonel."

31

"My profound regrets." Hom nodded, his slender face revealing nothing.

"Europa fever. I felt the onset last week"—Rayburn's smile grew brittle—"several days after I took office. Sundberg has verified my condition. Not that I didn't know; that plague has been the bane of that world, Hom."

"Is there no cure?"

"None," he declared flatly. "I have two weeks to live, if that long. Three at most. That again makes the problem of succession imperative."

"A grievous duty," Hom agreed.

"I'm stuck with the same problem Wehl had. I can't name Franckel or Montre or even Gullen without having the empire torn apart. Neither can I appoint one and have the other two assassinated." He stilled the agent with a gesture. "Oh, I know, it has been done, but I hope we're growing more civilized."

"Man creeps starward by the inch," Hom observed.

"Nicely put." Rayburn leaned toward him. "That leaves but one alternative. I have to reappoint Wehl."

"He's seventy-six," Hom reflected.

Rayburn's eyes blazed briefly. "He's recovered from his mental stress," he reprimanded. "He knows this empire as no other man ever has, Hom. Certainly he'll have sufficient time to reappoint a proper successor."

Hom inclined his head.

"Wehl was a great premier," Rayburn continued. "History will regard him as one of the best. Oh, I know, many regarded him as a tyrant, but how else can such a vast empire be held together? The soft premiers of the past didn't last."

"Craxton Wehl wasn't soft."

"But great," Rayburn persisted. "He brought great technological and cultural advancements. Have you seen the *papier-mâché* redwoods up north? Absolutely waterproof. They'll be standing there for longer than the originals. The fact is trivial, but it symbolizes the point I am trying to make. Wehl had a keen sense of history."

"He was unique," Hom reflected. Rayburn smiled, thinking the agent's remark could be interpreted in many ways. But Hom hadn't gotten to where he was by putting the wrong foot forward.

"That brings us to our immediate problem," the premier

continued. He fluttered his big hands. "Wehl has vanished."

"From the sky clinic?"

"Into nowhere," he affirmed, "or so it appears."

"Magic is the process of the commonplace."

"What kind of magic?" Rayburn lifted his head. "Sundberg has but four people in the clinic, all staff. He put the electrode to each of them. They're clean. Kidnapping or connivance is out."

"Did he put the electrode to himself?"

Rayburn smiled mirthlessly. "We can eliminate him. He knows it's his neck if he doesn't get Wehl back. He's hired private intelligence to do the job—a fellow named Felix Quigg."

"Expensive," Hom murmured.

"Is he good?"

"To whoever buys."

"That kind, eh? You'd better watch him."

"Of a certainty." The agent's gaze sharpened. "What's Sundberg's surmise?"

"He believes Wehl teleported."

"Ah!"

"Far-fetched, eh?"

"I find nothing far-fetched in this universe," Hom observed.

"Including Wehl's ability to teleport?"

"Surprising, yes, but not unbelievable." Hom tilted his head with a quick birdlike movement. "There is nothing in Wehl's background to indicate such a power. Or perhaps I should say, nothing of record."

"Sundberg expressed the opinion that the power had been latent, that it had been freed during the course of the surgery. Strange things happen when you tinker with the brain." Rayburn contemplated the agent thoughtfully before continuing. "To complicate matters, the surgery left him amnesic. Sundberg feels certain that the condition is but temporary."

"He teleported in an amnesic condition?"

"Apparently."

Hom said carefully, "We know very little about teleportation. Isn't the capability supposedly limited to under five miles?"

"Not if Wehl teleported."

33

"We are told that a teleport must have a fixed destination—must know its exact parameters. Could Wehl manage that in an amnesic condition?"

"I put that question to Sundberg," Rayburn admitted. "He didn't know. Teleportation is still a dark secret. Its few practitioners don't give out much. Can a peeper peep when amnesic? The answer is yes, according to Sundberg. Perhaps the same applies to the teleport. Sundberg surmised that he must have resurrected a destination at the subconscious level. Is that possible? I don't know."

"The subconscious is a sea of mystery," the agent conceded. "I'll accept his disappearance as *de facto* and go on from there."

"Let's be blunt," Rayburn said. "It would be of great advantage to others—I'm thinking particularly of Franckel—if Wehl weren't returned. That would leave the Big Power Seat open at my death. He'd prefer the risk of a scramble to the certainty of another successor. It's quite possible that some action might be taken to prevent Wehl's return."

"Who knows he's missing?"

"Outside of the official family, only Felix Quigg. I don't have to tell you how saleable that information is. Once it gets out, a thousand plots will be born overnight, Hom. Everyone will be jockeying for the new power alignment, or trying to create one."

"Such attempts never cease," Hom said. His head moved up. "With your permission, I have one question."

"Speak," he ordered.

"Do you trust Dr. Sundberg?"

"Implicitly."

"Ah, yes." Hom gazed at the ceiling. The premier had the impression that he had withdrawn into some remote world of his own—that he was weighing, measuring, calculating. For some reason it made him think of the banks of computers in the opposite wing of the building. Hom's lids drooped, giving his eyes a hooded expression. Rayburn was certain that the agent's evaluations would be flattering to no one. Then Hom's eyes snapped open; dark and clear, they told nothing.

Rayburn said, "I've issued a Q order to isolate the clinic. No personal communications; it's being monitored to ensure compliance. No one can leave or enter, your agents

34

excepted. And Sundberg. Inasmuch as he's treating me, he will come here from time to time. Perhaps you'd better slap a Q order on Quigg. Better yet, take him into custody until this thing is cleared up."

"I'd prefer not to."

"Why?"

"He might lead us to Wehl."

"That's possible. I'll leave it up to you." Rayburn's voice grew sharp. "You have one week to get Wehl back."

"I'll act accordingly." Hom nodded politely and rose. When the door closed behind him, Rayburn stood, fighting to steady himself. The brief meeting had drained him of every ounce of energy. But he couldn't allow anyone to suspect how weak he really was. Too much was at stake.

But Felix Quigg knew! Damn Sundberg, he had panicked. Because he had, a dangerous game had become far more dangerous. Quigg was completely unscrupulous, a man who sold to the higest bidder. Hom had verified that. Now Quigg possessed a secret that was worth a fortune. Did he realize that? Of course he did. But that was just one hazard. A small one, really.

He extended his hands, flexed them, gazed at the corded muscles of his arms. He looked to be a perfect physical specimen. He laughed mirthlessly. He was dying. Each day he grew weaker; death was coming fast. For how long could he conceal the gravity of his condition? Not for long.

Wehl had to be found! He clenched his hands tightly. If Quigg didn't find him, Hom would. But he had to be found soon. Craxton Wehl, the most publicized face in the Solar Empire—it seemed inconceivable that he could walk any street on Earth without being recognized. The thought was cheering.

He went to the window and gazed across the green lawn to the city's distant spires. If Sundberg's patient had teleported, to where had he teleported? The question was interesting. If Quigg or Hom found him, would he teleport again? Good Lord, the man could bounce around the continent like a grasshopper. He hadn't thought of that. How would one go about snaring a teleport? He hadn't thought to ask that of Hom. But Hom would know. Hom struck him as a man who knew everything. Everything?

How much did Hom know?

Leon Sobel, Hom's chief special investigator, listened intently as his superior spoke. His dark face, marred by a white scar that slashed downward across one cheek to pull the corner of his mouth slightly awry, held a surly look. His small, deep-set eyes showed nothing of his thoughts.

Hom finished the story, omitting nothing. "What's your reaction?" he asked.

"Rayburn's holding out. So is Sundberg."

"I believe so."

"Wehl a teleport, a victim of amnesia, and Rayburn dying—that's difficult to believe."

"People do teleport, people do lose their memories, and people do die," Hom observed. "We have to accept that at face value."

"Would Rayburn pass the power to a man suffering amnesia?"

"Sundberg is of the opinion that it's of the retrograde type, caused by the surgery," Hom explained. "He feels he can clear it up with the proper therapy."

Sobel stroked his jaw. "Suppose Wehl can't be found?"

"Translate that."

"Suppose he already has been disposed of?"

"We have to work on the assumption he's alive," Hom said.

"A living gold mine."

"Which Felix Quigg fully realizes."

"How many know about this?"

"Too many." Hom listed their names. "The secret won't keep."

Sobel grimaced. "What's my specialty?"

"Felix Quigg. He might lead you to Wehl."

"He'd more likely lead me to the highest buyer."

"I've considered that," Hom acknowledged.

"Sundberg's the boy with the answers."

"I've concluded that."

"I'd like to put him through the wringer," Sobel reflected.

"That's out. The premier has implicit trust in him."

"I haven't."

"Nor I, but we can't touch him."

Sobel said, "I can't see Rayburn's dying need of Wehl,

36

no pun intended. He could appoint a successor and make it stick."

"He wants Craxton Wehl, period," Hom declared.

"Wehl it is." Sobel sighed. "I still can't buy the story."

"I won't argue the point, but that doesn't enter into the job." Hom's eyes weighed his subordinate. "We have to return Wehl to the clinic within the week; that's our sole concern."

"A teleport with amnesia ... " Sobel lifted his hulking frame from the chair. "It's a crazy business."

"It's that," Hom agreed. Watching the other depart, he thought it the understatement of the year.

FOUR

He awoke, shivering and bewildered, his body filled with a vast ache. His head throbbed. The floor on which he lay was cold and hard. Gray light beyond the single window spoke of dawn. He jerked to a sitting position and looked around wildly.

Where am I? The question brought a quick dread. In the gloom he perceived a couch, a scattering of chairs, a table that held a vase of flowers. My God, he was ... Her apartment! Mura's! An anguished groan escaped him. He had been in jail, had fallen asleep on a narrow cot in the small barred cell; now he was here! Was he crazy?

He staggered to his feet, his mind dancing with the impossible. How? How? He'd been locked up—that much was clear. But when had he gotten out? How had he gotten here? He rubbed his face with his hands, then froze as he heard movement. A door creaked open and light flooded the room. A girl stood in the entrance, clasping a robe to her throat.

"You!" Her face held both incredulity and fright.

"Miss Breen," he croaked.

"How did you get in?" she demanded.

"I ... just woke up."

37

"In here?" Her face showed disbelief. He nodded, afraid to trust his voice. She ran to the door, twisted the knob, then whirled back toward him. "Locked!" she exclaimed.

"Locked?" He stared numbly at her.

"How did you get in?"

"I don't know," he whispered.

"Something is terribly wrong." She wet her lips nervously.

"I was in jail. I went to sleep in a cell."

"And woke up here?"

"Just now," he affirmed.

"I must be going crazy," she whispered.

"No, it's something else."

"What?"

"I don't know," he confessed.

She gazed around helplessly. "A man can't come in through the walls or ceiling or floor. Perhaps the same people who brought you here the first time brought you again. That has to be it; they could have picked the lock."

"Perhaps," he answered dubiously.

"Why were you in jail?"

"I was sleeping in the park."

"Did . . . they find out your name?"

"Gerald Sundberg. I'm Gerald Sundberg."

"How did they find out?"

"It just came to me."

"While you were in jail?"

"When the policeman asked me," he explained.

"Did you remember anything else—your address, family, anything at all?"

He shook his head.

"Didn't the police ask?"

"I couldn't remember anything else."

"That's frightening."

"I'll go away. I won't bother you any more."

"No." She forced a smile. "You'd leave me wondering, always wondering. I'd never quite know whether or not I was crazy. You have to stay, at least until we find out."

"You're not crazy. Perhaps I am, but you're not."

"You're not crazy either," she answered quietly. "Something strange has happened but there has to be an answer. Perhaps if you stay, someone will come to get you."

"Who?"

38

"Whoever brought you here."

"But wouldn't I have known?"

"Perhaps it's your memory," she suggested. "Perhaps it blanks out from time to time. I've heard of such things."

"I don't believe so," he replied.

"Neither do I, not really." She forced the smile back to her lips. "You look utterly fatigued. Rest and I'll make some coffee. It'll do you good. It'll do us both good," she added.

"Thank you." He sank down on the couch. How had he gotten here? No one had brought him; he felt certain of that. Although her surmise seemed logical, he knew it wasn't true. His conscious memory, while scarcely a day old, had functioned clearly since his first awakening. He could account for every moment until the instant he'd fallen asleep in the cell. How had he gotten out? He'd find out, he vowed. He clenched his fists, feeling them tremble.

She returned with the coffee, handed him a cup, and sat across from him. The hot liquid scalded his tongue, but he savored the bitter taste. She watched him quietly.

"Perhaps after you rest," she said musingly.

"Perhaps what?"

"Perhaps you'll remember."

"I have to remember!"

"The loss of memory isn't uncommon."

He smiled ruefully. "Not at my age."

"It isn't necessarily age," she remonstrated. "Many things cause amnesia. Have you heard of a *fugue?*"

"That's mental, isn't it?"

"A flight from reality." She nodded. "It happens occasionally. Life becomes unbearable and a person simply flees—pulls down a blind over his conscious memories, goes elsewhere, starts life anew. But it's not a conscious act. It's like the mind itself shut a door, closing off the reality of the past. It's like being born anew."

"With an ancient body." He grimaced.

"Youth is a mental state, not physical," she reprimanded.

"To youth, perhaps, but the aches and pains tell me otherwise. I need oil."

"The mind is the most important," she persisted.

"You seem to know quite a bit about it," he observed.

"I used to teach."

39

"On Mars?"

She nodded. "The Noachis school. Our dome looked out over Mare Serpentis, the Serpentine Sea." Her face took on a wistful look. "It was ochre and orange and, oh, so lovely. At high noon the sun was a gold, gold ball pasted against a blue-black sky. You never see such a sky from Earth."

She spoke of the Grissom mountains, scarlet and red against the darkness beyond, and of empty sinks of red clay that seemingly stretched into infinity. It was in such a sink, she said, that early colonists had discovered a scattering of artifacts of a long-vanished civilization; time had cloaked its identity.

Her face glistened. As the words tumbled out, he sensed something of which she spoke—the awesome grandeur of a dead, dead world which a handful of colonists were attempting to revive. The bleak plains, the two strange moons that hurtled through its skies, the cities taking form in its bowels—they came alive in his mind. Then suddenly he was aware that she had stopped speaking.

He asked, "Why did you return to Earth?"

Pain filled her eyes. "My mother was born here. After my father died she grew despondent, wanted to return." She told haltingly of the difficulty in trying to adjust to life on Earth after the freedom they'd known on Mars. Nor had Earth been as her mother had remembered it. Her friends were gone, scattered; they'd found themselves in a strange land. Her mother had died the previous year. By then their scant savings were gone; now Mura was locked to Earth.

"What do you do?" he asked sympathetically.

"Assembly work in a factory."

"If you're a teacher?"

She tossed her head. "They don't approve of Martian teachers on Earth. I couldn't get a job. I wasn't sufficiently indoctrinated in their Wehlistic philosophy."

"That man is a servant of men?" Voicing the question, he wondered from what deep well he'd drawn it. The quote had come almost as a reflex.

"The servant of a machine," she corrected. "That's the reality of it." She spoke disdainfully. On Earth the machine commanded; all lives were built around it. Man had surrendered, perhaps unknowingly, until he existed solely as a part of a system too great for him to grasp. He had become nothing but a body, a muscle, a unit of energy geared to perform a certain task. "You can thank your Craxton Wehl for that," she said.

"Craxton Wehl?" He felt a stirring.

"You don't remember? He's the former premier." She tossed her head again to signify her disapproval. "He considered people as cattle—all but the powerful and wealthy. Oh, I know, he created technical universities, but they were geared to the technical skills required to maintain his automatic society. But not even the technicians and managers who operate it are free; or at least their freedom is a relative thing. If a man can't think, he can't question; it's as easy as that."

"There's always room for the individual," he protested.

"On Mars, yes, and the other OutSat worlds, but not here." Her eyes arched. "They say he went crazy."

"Craxton Wehl?"

"That's why he gave up the power. Oh, he was twisted, all right." She smiled bitterly.

"I'm sorry you had to return to Earth."

"I was happy to bring my mother back. She hated it there." She caught his surprised look and rushed on, "Not everyone likes Mars, not even among the second and third generations. It's not a planet about which one can be complacent. You either love it or hate it. My father and I loved it; my mother hated it."

"Why was that?"

"The stillness," she said simply. "Oh, the domes were filled with life, but it was the stillness of the planet itself. It had died eons before man's arrival. That's what she felt—not the life in the domes but the stillness of the planet. We have a term for it on Mars: we call it 'the Great Silence.' To her, it was stifling. Now and then, rarely, there was a dust storm. She used to wait for them, just to see the movement."

"I can sense her feelings," he agreed.

"You can't imagine such a stillness," she denied. "You live in a world of motion."

"Tell me."

Her voice fell to a whisper. Beyond the domes was no motion whatever—no life, no waving grasses, no trees to bend in the wind. There were no brooks, no restless seas,

41

no bird in those beautiful velvet skies. She had known of such things only from the books and films and tapes shipped in from Earth, but her mother had known them from memory. That was far more poignant. Her mother couldn't see the beauty of Mars, but only what it didn't have. "The outer world held the stillness of a painting," she said.

"I've heard that." He felt the stirring of memory again, and wondered.

"Once my mother called, 'Come quickly!' I followed her out into the central dome, wondering what had happened. She pointed toward the arched vault overhead and cried, 'Look!' I saw a thin white thread against the sky. It was a cloud, the first I'd seen, and I was fourteen. Urged by the wind, changing shape, it moved slowly out over Mare Serpentis. Everyone in the dome had stopped to watch. No one moved or whispered. Finally the cloud was lost to sight. It never came again."

"You make Mars sound quite bleak," he observed.

"I'm telling you of the Mars my mother saw," she countered. "It wasn't that way at all." She spoke wistfully of going outside the dome with her father, out into the stillness, the quiet. They'd drive toward the broken country of the Grissom mountains, exploring as they went. Red slabs stabbed against the sky; yellow chasms split the ground. The world was a rock garden in vivid hues, and no people; none at all.

"Perhaps that was it," she whispered. "It made a person feel like something special."

"I can understand that feeling," he agreed.

"You can?"

"Man is more than clay, Mura."

"I didn't think they understood that here." Her eyes blazed. "This world is like a womb. It provides everything; you fight for nothing."

"Except to be an individual."

"How many people are interested in that?" she demanded scornfully.

"Perhaps more than you think."

"You'd better rest." She rose abruptly, went into the next room, and closed the door. It struck him that he'd understood her perfectly—both her love of Mars and her scorn of Earth. Yet he knew she was wrong. Walled in by a

42

closed environment, her view followed a narrow perspective. That was quite understandable.

He lay on the couch and stared upward at the ceiling. Was he really Gerald Sundberg? The name created no stir in his mind. A name was an ego property, he mused; as a symbol of the self, it should scream its existence. But the name Gerald Sundberg screamed nothing; it was merely a name.

After a while he slept.

Mura returned from work early, her face excited. She clasped an afternoon paper. "There's a story," she said nervously.

"About me?" He felt a touch of panic.

"Your escape." She spread the paper on the table. "There!" She pointed to a column she had outlined in pencil. The headline read: PRISONER ESCAPES CITY JAIL.

He hurriedly scanned the account. Arrested under the name of Gerald Sundberg, he had mysteriously vanished from his cell shortly before dawn. *Police were unable ...* He finished and looked up, his mind awed. "How did I do it?" he whispered.

"I don't know." She wet her lips. "But there's more. You're not Gerald Sundberg. At least I don't believe you are."

"I'm not?" He felt the stillness of isolation again—the sensation of a rudderless ship in a turbulent sea.

"There are only two Gerald Sundbergs listed in Information Central," she told him. "One is a lawyer, the other a doctor. I called the lawyer. He was there."

"The doctor?"

"He runs a sky clinic. I looked him up in the medical directory; he's only forty-three."

"Not Gerald Sundberg." He gazed askance at her.

"We'll find out who you are," she encouraged.

"Couldn't I have come from somewhere else?"

"It's possible."

"I have to have a name!" he cried. "I'm keeping it!"

"There might be a way to find out for certain."

"How?"

"A peeper."

He shook his head. "Peepers cost money."

43

"I know where there's a partial," she declared. "He might help, at least tell you who you are. He's not licensed so he'd be cheap. A girl at work told me about him."

"I don't know," he mumbled. The idea of someone looking into his mind was frightening.

"We have to try," she persisted. "I'll get the details."

"But I haven't got a charge plate."

"We could use mine; we could offer what I can afford. If he's as they say, he'll be glad to get it."

"As they say?" He eyed her questioningly.

"They say he's been sentenced to social reform several times for petty crimes," she explained. "He can't get regular work."

"Could a partial peep an amnesic mind?"

"We have to try," she urged.

"If you say." He sighed wearily. Anything seemed better than not knowing.

That night, staring into the darkness, he thought again of her words and felt a terrible loneliness—the loneliness of a man without a name. Of all the teeming millions around him, he alone had no identity, none whatever—no milestones by which he could gauge the course of his life. He had come from nowhere, was here, was going ... *where?* The future seemed as empty as the past.

He had to be Gerald Sundberg! He clung fiercely to the hope. At least he had to have a name! Somewhere were people who knew him, perhaps even now were searching for him. A man couldn't go through sixty or seventy years without leaving an identifiable trail. Could a man walk through life without leaving a footprint? The thought that possibly he could was chilling.

Perhaps the peeper could help him. Perhaps he could tear aside that strange gray veil that cloaked his mind, draw forth the fragments from which he could resurrect his past. But the peeper was only a partial, an incomplete telepath; he could but skim the surface of a mind. And if he failed?

Why then he'd try something else—he'd never stop trying. Never! A man had a right to know who he was. Even a wretched name, a wretched station in life, was better than no name at all. It was the most cherished thing a man had, for it alone gave him identity as an individual. Did Mura understand that? Contemplating her concern

44

and willingness to help him, he decided that perhaps she did. Neither, when he thought of it, was he alone.

He had Mura.

FIVE

Mura peered at the faded numerals above the entrance to an old apartment building. In the dim glare of a nearby street lamp, they were scarcely discernible. "This is the place," she said in a hushed voice. "He lives in apartment five."

Sundberg—as he had come to think of himself—nodded jerkily, wondering again why he'd ever agreed to consult the peeper. Especially a peeper like Obie Frye, if he were to judge by the dismal neighborhood in which the man lived. Certainly the littered streets, dilapidated buildings, and the few people he'd glimpsed moving furtively among the shadows did little to allay his doubts. But Mura's presence was comforting. He had to admire the way she'd taken him in hand, was helping him to find himself again.

He followed her into a narrow hallway that stank of cooking odors. The jangle of music and occasional voices came through the thin walls. Mura found the apartment she was seeking and knocked. Movement came from inside. The door swung open and an unkempt man nearing middle age stared at them from deep-sunken eyes. His face, narrow and bony, badly needed shaving.

"Mr. Frye?" she asked. At his nod she said hurriedly, "I'm the person who . . ."

"Come in," he interrupted. The nasal quality of his voice grated on Sundberg's ears. Frye stepped aside to let them enter. "This the fellow who wants to get peeped?"

"He has amnesia," she explained.

"Blanked out, eh?"

"I want to know who I am," he said defiantly.

"You look familiar." Frye stared at him.

45

"I do?" He felt a wild hope. Mura had said the same thing.

"Something about your nose and mouth." Frye edged slowly around to the side, studying him from various angles. "I'm almost certain of it."

"Who do you think I am?" he asked hopefully.

"I didn't say I knew. I said you looked familiar." Frye eyed Mura reflectively. "A peep should do it. That'll be a hundred cpu's."

"A hundred?" Dismay flooded her face. "I haven't got that much."

"Then why'd you come here?"

"I thought perhaps . . ."

"That you could beat me down?" he interrupted.

Sundberg straightened his thin shoulders and said coldly, "We'd better leave."

"But we have to find out," she protested.

"How much can you pay?" Frye demanded.

"Twenty-five cpu's."

"Twenty-five?"

"That's all I can afford," she replied firmly.

"How about him?" Frye gestured with a thumb.

"I haven't got a charge plate," he answered weakly.

"No charge plate?" The peeper peered at him.

"I must have lost it. I can't remember."

"Can't remember nothin'?"

"Not since I awakened."

"You can't expect much of a peep for twenty-five cpu's," Frye growled.

"If you could just tell him who he is," Mura begged.

"A name?" asked Frye cannily. "You want a name?"

"I'm Gerald Sundberg. I remember that."

"Sounds familiar." Frye squinted at him, then straightened alertly. "Say, aren't you the fellow who escaped from jail?"

"I was sleeping in the park," he admitted.

"How'd you break out?"

"I don't know."

"You can tell me." Frye smiled craftily. "A peeper's like a doctor; everything's confidential. Did you bribe the jailer?"

"I don't know."

46

"The amnesia comes and goes," Mura interrupted. "He can't remember what happened."

"Mighty convenient." Frye snickered.

"It's the truth," he blurted. "I just woke up and I was back in her apartment."

"Hers?"

"She's trying to help me," he explained edgily. "I can't see why you have to know all that."

"It opens your mind, makes the peepin' easier."

"Please peep him," Mura urged. "Here, I have my charge plate." She drew it from her purse, set the punch key at twenty-five cpu, and handed it to him. He drew an imprinter from his pocket, inserted it over a transfer of funds check, and pressed down on the handle. Inspecting the check, he handed her the carbon.

"Sit down," he instructed Sundberg. He pulled over a lamp. "Open your mind."

"Open it?" Sundberg blinked under the blazing light.

"Keep it blank."

"The light blinds me."

"Look a bit off to one side and don't think of anything. Relax, keep your mind blank." Frye stared down at him. "Relax as if you were falling asleep."

"I'm trying."

"Don't talk, just relax." Frye's voice droned on soothingly. For a moment Sundberg's consciousness was filled with the peeper's odious presence, the shabby room, Mura standing worriedly off to one side; but gradually the imagery faded and the faint jangle of music from down the hall died away. His lids grew heavy and he let them close, grateful to escape the penetrating light. Colored after-images floated through his mind.

"Relax, relax." Frye's voice came from afar. He's trying to hypnotize me, Sundberg thought dreamily. Peace, quiet, solitude—he had the eerie sensation of floating in a midnight sea. No sun, no moon, no stars—nothing save the engulfing blackness of infinity, the timelessness of eternity.

"His mind's blank." The peeper's voice was a ghostly whisper.

"Can't you get anything?" Mura, he thought dreamily.

"Nothing."

"Please keep trying."

"No memories . . . none at all."

47

The last words jolted him. Jerking violently, he fought his way back to consciousness. As his lids snapped open, he recoiled from the harsh light. "A man has to have memories," he shouted. "They're there, somewhere."

"You have none," Frye snapped.

"For God's sake, peep me again," he cried. A man with no memories! The fear surged through him. A man with no identity was bad; a man with no memories was a thousand times worse.

"It would take a week."

"Try again," Mura implored.

"For twenty-five cpu's?" Frye sneered.

"I must have a charge plate!" Sundberg exclaimed. "I have to have one somewhere! How could I have lived? I couldn't have gotten to this age without one; you know that."

"No use." Frye shook his head.

"No use," he echoed hollowly. He rose heavily, gripped with despair. If a peeper couldn't tell him who he was, who could? Someone had to know! A man of sixty or seventy couldn't walk unseen and unheard throughout the years. He would have left records in ten thousand places. He had to have memories, a whole storehouse of them. They were there, somewhere, waiting to be freed. At times he could all but sense them, small shadows that reeled swiftly through the corridors of his mind, racing just beyond his grasp. He smiled bravely at Mura.

"We'll find out," she encouraged.

"Perhaps," Frye observed dubiously.

"How can my mind be blank?" he cried angrily. "How could I know what I'm doing, where I am? How could I think if my mind were blank?

"Your thinking is limited to the past few days."

"But the past is there," he protested. "I have to draw from the past to know the things I know."

"What things?"

"Feelings of recognition, like when I look at the tower at the space terminal, or when I'm in Mura's apartment. I sense things when I look at Glade Avenue—at its shops and dwellings. Even the name rings in my mind. Things tug at my memory."

"Have you ever lived around here?"

"How would I know?"

"Of course he has memories," Mura put in quickly. "The amnesia masks them. Isn't that it?"

"Could be." Frye looked dubious.

"I remember the fish eye," he blurted.

"Fish eye?" Mura gazed at him.

"Nightmare," he answered sheepishly.

"What kind of a nightmare?" demanded Frye.

"Everything's distorted, like looking through the bulbous bottom of a glass bowl," he explained. "I guess that's why I think of it as looking through a fish eye."

"What do you see?"

"A twisted universe of gigantic burning stars."

"Do you hit the needle?"

"Of course he doesn't," Mura cried angrily.

"Sounds like needle-talk to me," Frye said. "Either that or you're pounding the pills."

"You're wrong," she said coldly.

Frye snickered. "I've had those nightmares."

"Let's go," said Sundberg wearily. He grasped her arm, steering her toward the door. At the front entrance he glanced back. The peeper stood in the hallway watching them.

"He's horrid," Mura cried wrathfully. "I'm sorry we went there."

"I don't believe him," he said defiantly.

"Amnesia is not uncommon," she stated. "It often passes as quickly as it comes."

"I hope so." He looked at the quarter moon rising above the rooftops. Sallow in a murky sky, it brought the dim recollection of past moons sailing through shadowy space. The stars were dim and yellow, as if soiled by the polluted air through which he viewed them. Nothing like the universe he saw through the fish eye! He shivered.

But it wasn't just the moon. Buildings, streets, sounds, the glowing lights of an occasional aircar—everything spoke hauntingly of a familiar past now buried beneath an avalanche of years. Although he couldn't discern its dimensions, he was aware of its existence—a past when he had seen and felt and known the same world through which he now walked as a stranger. How could that be? It was part of the mystery which ensnared him.

He said confidently, "I'll discover who I am."

"Of course you will," she agreed.

"I have a name; that's a start."

"Whoever dropped you knows." She cast him a sidelong glance. "Mr. Frye thought you looked familiar."

"He wasn't certain."

"No, but I've had the same feeling. Perhaps you resemble someone I once knew."

"Why did I escape into amnesia?" He caught her quick glance and continued, "Amnesia is an escape, isn't it? You said so once. Then from what was I escaping?"

"It also can be caused by shock," she answered gently.

"A physical shock?"

"That, too."

"I hope that was it. I'd hate to think I was running away from myself."

"I'm certain you weren't."

"Why do you say that?"

"You're not the kind of a man who'd run away from himself."

"How can I know?" he cried. Gazing at the dismal neighborhood, he wondered how he could penetrate the veil, see the yesteryears that had gone into his making. Good or bad, he had to know them. He had to be somebody; not just Gerald Sundberg, a name, but someone with a living past. He had to look back through the long corridor of years, pick up the threads of his being. Only by doing that could he become a whole man again. He would do it, and no one would stop him. A fierce determination assailed him.

Straightening his thin shoulders, he strode more briskly at her side.

"Mr. Quigg?"

About to enter his office, Felix Quigg turned. A man nearing middle age was peering at him through deepsunken eyes. His narrow, bony face had a servile expression. Quigg coolly took in the unkempt dress and shabby shoes. "Yes?"

"I have some information to sell," the man whined.

"See my secretary," Quigg snapped. He reached for the door.

"It's about Gerald Sundberg."

He turned back, suddenly alert. "Sundberg?"

"The fellow who escaped from the jail."

"Oh, that Sundberg." He suppressed his excitement. He'd had no doubt whatever about the prisoner's identity, or about his method of escape. Not that he'd enlightened the police, but he had spread quite a net of his own.

"The talk along the street is that you'd pay for information," the other said hopefully.

"What's your name?"

"Frye ... Obie Frye."

"Come into my office, Frye." Quigg led him to his private sanctum, closed the door behind them, and gestured toward a chair. Frye sat gingerly. Quigg sat at his desk, deliberately fussing with some papers to keep the other on edge. Finally he pushed the papers aside and looked up. "Now what's this about Sundberg?"

"They said you'd pay," Frye blurted worriedly.

"Pay for what? Come, man, you haven't told me anything yet. Speak up!"

"I can tell you how to find him."

"You know where he is?"

"Not exactly." Frye shifted uncomfortably.

"What do you know?"

"He came to me for help."

"He came to you?" Quigg eyed him disbelievingly. "Why would he do that?"

"I'm a peeper," Frye answered sullenly.

"You, a peeper? Don't try to klotch me," Quigg cried angrily. "There are only half a dozen peepers in this part of the country and I know them all. What's your game?"

"I'm a partial. I was sentenced to social reform so I can't get a license."

"You couldn't get one anyway, not a partial." Quigg smiled narrowly. "They'd slap you back there if they caught you peeping."

"You can't prove nothin'," Frye flared. He tried to conceal his fright.

"Who said I was trying to prove anything? I'm stating a point of law."

"I ain't breaking no law!"

"You are if you're peeping." Quigg gestured airily. "But we'll let that go. What did you read in his mind?"

"Nothin'."

"Nothing?"

"It was blank," Frye admitted.

"He has amnesia."

"He told me, but I heard you can peep those birds."

"So they say." Quigg studied the other curiously. Frye's dress and manner were that of the born loser, and the man knew it. But he'd been born a winner, if his words were true. How could he have thrown away such a gift? He asked, "Are you peeping me?"

Frye shook his head sullenly.

"You're trying," he challenged.

"I'm only a partial, Mr. Quigg. I told you that."

"You need peace and quiet, eh?"

"I have to study 'em for a while," Frye admitted.

"How did Sundberg know about you?"

"A woman brought him."

"What woman?"

"Well . . ."

"Speak up, man!"

"Why?" Frye demanded belligerantly. "You haven't paid me anything yet."

"Ten cpu," Quigg snapped.

"As much as you want that guy?"

"He's not that important." He shrugged. "A minor case, really."

"You brought me into your office fast enough when I told you about him," Frye challenged. "You're trying to beat me down."

Quigg eyed him imperturbably. "I'll go twenty, that's tops."

"I'll go somewhere else." Frye stood up.

"You know someone else who's buying?"

"I've got my lines out," he answered evasively. "Besides, if he's not important, why'd the police grab him?"

"Sleeping in the park."

"How about the jail break? They'd sure want him for that."

"Sit down," Quigg snapped. Watching the other slide back into the seat, he weighed his thoughts. A peeper, even a partial, could prove a gold mine if properly used. Clean him up, get him a haircut and new clothes and he'd look fairly presentable. If he could get him into a position

52

to peep the real Sundberg or Madelyn Wehl . . . or Craxton Wehl! Do that and the wind would hit the money tree!

He caught Frye's eyes and held them while he leaned back and made a Gothic arch with his fingers. The peeper shifted uneasily under his gaze. Quigg veiled his eyes, watching the other's discomfort grow. Abruptly he said, "I have a proposition. If you produce, the sky's the limit."

"How much?" asked Frye edgily.

"Two hundred."

"What do I have to do?"

"A small peep job."

"Who?" Frye demanded worriedly. "I can't take chances."

"Oh, it'll be safe enough."

"Who?"

"I'm not quite certain."

"Well . . ."

"I'll throw a new suit, shoes, and a haircut into the bargain," Quigg put in quickly. "If things work out, I might have a lot more work for you. A small job here, another there—you can't laugh off an opportunity like that, man. The street's loaded with people who'd grab at the chance."

"Yeah, but they can't peep minds."

"Quite true," Quigg murmured. He smiled cynically. "This is your lucky day, Frye. 'When in Time of Need, You Need Quigg and Associates'—that's one of our slogans. We're the biggest in the business, but I suppose you know that. Telepaths? I have them knocking at my door every day, but I'm selective. I demand absolute loyalty. Is that too much to ask? I don't believe so, yet it's a difficult thing to find. Ethical standards are out the window, Frye; that's the tragedy of our age."

"That's true," Frye smirked.

"Did you ever hear the story of the man who wandered the streets with a laser lamp searching for an honest man?" Quigg sighed. "He never found him. That was ages ago, but it's gotten worse since. Most people would sell their own mother for five cpu."

"I wouldn't," Frye exclaimed hastily.

"Ten cpu?"

"I'm not . . ." Frye looked into the other's eyes and

53

suddenly understood. "Well, if it were part of the job," he added weakly.

"I believe you'll do." Quigg rubbed his hands briskly. "As it happens, I do have a small job."

SIX

He awoke, his head throbbing, his body filled with an intolerable ache. He struggled to a sitting position and felt a wave of nausea; the room swam giddily around him. He blinked, trying to bring his eyes into focus. God, what was wrong with him? The thought that he might die before he could discover who he was brought a stab of terror. A man couldn't die a stranger even to himself. That thought was chilling.

The peeper! He remembered Obie Frye's bony, unshaven face, the deep-sunken eyes and unkempt dress—Frye's claim that his mind was a blank! He was nobody; that's what Frye had claimed. *Nobody! Nobody! Nobody!* The word clamored in his mind. He gazed at his hands; they were shaking.

Frye was wrong; he'd prove it! He'd find out who he was today! He straightened, cocking his head to listen. The apartment was silent. He gazed in dismay at the window. The angle of the sun told him it was late afternoon; he'd slept through the night and most of the day. He winced at the lost hours.

He slipped from the couch and dressed hurriedly. Going to the bathroom, he gazed at his reflection in the mirror. He looked old and haggard. His face had a wizened, unhealthy appearance, as if cast from yellow wax. But it was the face of . . . *somebody!* That was the thing; the face in the mirror had identity. *He was Gerald Sundberg!* Frye couldn't deprive him of that.

He found a note from Mura directing him to get breakfast. She cared! He folded it carefully and slipped it into his pocket. While eating, he planned what he might do in the brief time that remained before evening. Perhaps he could reach the Hall of Records before it closed, find a birth certificate for Gerald Sundberg. That would be a starter. Oh, there were all kinds of records. The prospects appeared boundless. Unless . . .

He straightened slowly. Unless he hadn't come from this area! If not, what then? But he had to have come from this area! The proof was there, buried deep in his mind. It came in the form of fleeting memories, feelings, subconscious knowledge. Once, long ago, he had walked these same streets.

He went outside and gazed at the old buildings. The recognition prickled at his mind. It was the feeling of viewing a yellowed photograph from long ago. The buildings were like that—yellowed and old. Fixing them in his mind, he closed his eyes; the image remained, then gradually changed. The stores and apartments appeared newer, the street cleaner. And down on the corner was a candy store. The candy store!

His eyes jerked open. There had been a candy store! He could all but smell the scent of chocolate, picture the old white-haired man who ran it. *Krant,* that was the name! Mr. Krant! Trembling, he started toward the corner, fearful of what he might find.

No candy store! Dismayed, he stared at the spot where he had remembered it. Now it was occupied by a sleazy shop selling cheap clothes. He closed his eyes tightly, trying to recapture the vision, but the candy store had evaporated; Mr. Krant's face had receded back into the dark places of his mind.

He entered the shop apprehensively. A sallow-faced clerk came toward him. "Could I be of help?"

"I'd like to speak to the manager."

The clerk eyed his shabby dress. "What about?"

"What is it?" An older man moved toward him from behind a counter.

"I was looking for a man who used to run a candy store here," he explained.

"Candy store?" The other rubbed his hands.

"His name was Krant."

"Oh!" The manager wrestled with his memory. "Krant's candy store was here many years ago. Krant must be dead now."

"Thank you!" he exclaimed gratefully. He retreated jubilantly to the street. Krant's candy store had been there! That proved that it wasn't his imagination, that he wasn't crazy. The structures erected in his mind had existed in the reality of cement and plastic and glass. How much else might he remember?

He turned to look at the sign. Krant's store had been there, only it had become Martin's Men's Shop. Time brought new faces, he thought. Small wonder memory was difficult. He cast a look at the brazen sky and started toward midtown.

As he reached Craxton Wehl Park, memory of his arrest brought a quick caution. He glanced around nervously. Aside from a few oldsters conversing as they watched the mechanical pigeons, the square was nearly deserted. He saw no sign of the cop.

He'd nearly reached the other side when he heard footsteps behind him and glanced back. Two tough-faced men were rapidly closing in on him. He moved faster, the fear heavy in his throat. Why should they be following him? Imagination, he thought, yet knew it wasn't. The knowledge brought a cold sweat. Abruptly he started to run.

A stinging pain between his shoulder blades staggered him. A dizzy sensation swept him, and his legs began to buckle. He felt his arms grasped from either side.

"Take it easy," a voice hissed "You're sick."

"I'm not," he cried. As he struggled to free himself, the hands gripped him more tightly.

"Quiet, old man."

"Let me go!"

"Shut up," the other snarled.

His mind reeling, Sundberg ceased his struggles, aware of a numbness pervading his body. The park, the trees, the buildings beyond—everything whirled in his visual field as if he were standing at the center of a vast pinwheel. He had the impression of an aircar landing in the square alongside him, then felt himself being half-carried, half-dragged.

"Get in," a voice rasped.

The police, he thought, they'd found him. The old man felt himself flung forward onto a seat. Someone scrambled in alongside him, followed by the vertiginous sensation of the vehicle being propelled upward.

"No, no, no . . ." The words were torn from his lips in a strangled sob. What was happening? They couldn't stop him now. He felt the vertigo again, the reeling of his mind. He was trying to fight it when he blacked out.

"One, two, three, four . . .
"Listen, listen, listen, listen . . ."
He struggled back toward consciousness, the words dinning in his ears. A sharp outburst of music jarred him, followed by the violent twanging of a steel guitar. A horn blared.
"One, two, three, four . . .
"Listen, listen, listen, listen . . . "
He fought against the blackness, trying to shut out the raucous noise. My God, where was he? He had a fleeting memory of the episode in the park. The discordant scream of the music came again, causing his nerves to vibrate. They felt like hot, taut wires. The music rose to a piercing wail that abruptly ceased.

The guitar twanged.

The horn blared.

"One, two, three, four . . ."
His eyes snapped open; he stared upward at a white ceiling. A white ceiling, white walls, a white sheet covering his body; the strong odor of disinfectant stung his nostrils.

"Listen, listen, listen, listen . . ."
"Shut it off!" he screamed. He attempted to block the words from his mind as he struggled to sit up, then discovered he was strapped to the bed. Shouting, he strained against his bonds. A door opened and a nurse in a white uniform peered in, then vanished.

"Come back! Come back!" he cried. The guitar twanged. The horn blared. "Come back! Come back!" Terror filled him as he fought to free himself.

The door popped open again and a white-gowned man entered, striding purposefully toward the bed.

"Who are you?" he screamed.

"My name is Doctor Meador. You've been sick."

"I'm not sick," he cried. "Why does everyone say I am?"

57

The guitar twanged.

"Quiet." Meador pushed him gently back against the sheet and brought out a stethoscope. "Do you remember your name?"

"Gerald Sundberg!" he shouted. "I'm Gerald Sundberg!"

"Ah, Mr. Sundberg." Meador listened to Sundberg's heart, then beamed a light first into one eye and then the other, examining the retinas. When he finished, Sundberg struggled to sit up.

"Where am I?" he demanded. For the first time he became aware of a nattily attired, sharp-featured man scrutinizing him from inside the door. A nurse peered in through the opening. "Where am I?" he shouted again.

"One, two, three, four . . ."

The sharp-featured man glanced at the nurse. "Shut that damned thing off," he barked. He swung back toward the bed. Sundberg watched him apprehensively.

"Who are you?" he croaked.

"Felix Quigg of Felix Quigg and Associates." A tailored smile appeared on the sharp face. "You've been ill, Mr. Wehl."

"Wehl?" He jerked upward against the straps. "Why do you call me by that name? I'm Gerald Sundberg!"

"No, you're Craxton Wehl." Quigg motioned the doctor aside.

"I'm not!" he screamed. "You can't rob me of my name. I'm Gerald Sundberg."

Quigg sat on the edge of the bed and looked down at him. "Listen to me," he ordered crisply.

"Not if you try to tell me I'm someone else," he yelled.

"Your correct name is Craxton Wehl," Quigg insisted. "Gerald Sundberg is the name of your doctor. You are ill, Mr. Wehl. You suffered amnesia and fled from Sundberg's clinic. I was retained to find you."

"Craxton Wehl." He sensed a fleeting memory. Where had he heard that name? He looked up at Quigg. "Who retained you?"

Quigg hesitated briefly. "Your daughter," he said. "She's been worried sick about you."

"Daughter?" He felt a shock.

"Madelyn. Don't you remember her?"

He shook his head dully. A daughter! He could scarcely

believe it, yet felt it must be true. He wasn't Gerald Sundberg at all; he was Craxton Wehl and he had a daughter! He accepted the knowledge stoically. Perhaps now his world would knit together again. He gazed at Quigg.

"Who am I?" he asked humbly.

"Craxton Wehl, just as I said."

"I mean, what did I do?"

"Oh!" Quigg's quick smile came again. "You are the former premier, Mr. Wehl. You left the Big Power Seat just before the, ah, onset of your amnesia."

"Premier?" he asked in a shocked voice.

"Of the Solar Empire."

"No! No!" He shook his head violently.

"You must accept that fact, Mr. Wehl."

"Oh, God!" He buried his face in his hands and shuddered. "I must be crazy!"

"Ill, Mr. Wehl, not crazy."

He looked up from his hands. "The former premier."

"One of the greatest," Quigg put in suavely. Wehl stared at him, thinking it must be a monstrous joke. But why would Quigg joke about a thing like that?

"Then I'm not Gerald Sundberg?" he whispered.

"No, you are Craxton Wehl. It's an honored name." Quigg straightened briskly. "I want you to try to remember everything about yourself."

"Remember?"

"Does the name Bernard Rayburn mean anything to you?"

"Bernard Rayburn?" Again he felt the brief tug of memory, a flaring of recognition that almost as quickly died. A tremor ran through his body. "I don't know," he muttered.

"Do you remember passing the power?"

"Passing the power?"

"When you stepped down in favor of Rayburn."

"I did that?" He felt a quick suspicion. "Why do you want to know?"

Quigg smiled pleasantly. "I'm attempting to induce total recall, Mr. Wehl. The proper questions might do it."

"I don't remember."

"The ceremony was held in the Sky Haven Clinic," Quigg prompted. "Does that ring a bell?"

He shook his head.

"Can't you remember anything?" Quigg asked sharply.

"The fish eye—I remember that."

"Fish eye?"

"Like staring at the universe through the bottom of a bulbous bowl," he explained. "Only the sky is different— it's as black as the pit of hell and the stars hang there like white diamonds, cold and harsh, yet curiously twisted; and then they're blotted out."

"Blotted out?"

"By a huge, fearful, distorted blob," he affirmed. Quigg glanced at the doctor, who nodded significantly.

"How often do you see that?"

"Looking through the fish eye? Not often." He searched his mind. "It's some kind of a nightmare."

"Do you remember being arrested?"

He said defiantly, "That was for sleeping in the park."

"But you remember it?"

"Yes." He nodded.

"How did you escape from jail, Mr. Wehl?"

"I can't remember." His eyes grew puzzled. "I just woke up and I wasn't there."

"What do you remember?" asked Quigg. "Try to think, search your mind. Tell me whatever comes to you."

"I remember the candy store."

"Candy store?" Quigg frowned.

"Mr. Krant's candy store. It was on the corner."

"Which corner?"

"Down the street from the apartment. On hot nights he'd leave the door open and you could smell the choco-late." He fluttered his hands helplessly. "But it's gone now; they sell clothes instead. Mr. Krant must be dead."

"What else do you remember?"

"The tower at the space terminal." He searched his memory. "The light on top of it goes around and around. Sometimes at night, when the aircars fly through it, they look like little silver moths."

"You mean now?"

"Now ... then." He gazed wonderingly at Quigg. "What is time? I don't know. Everything runs together in my mind. Is that because I have amnesia?"

"I'm trying to help you remember."

"Am I really Craxton Wehl?"

"Of course. Why do you ask?"

"The name doesn't make me feel anything."

"Does the name Gerald Sundberg?"

He thought about it. "Not really. What's going to happen to me?"

"I'm going to return you to your daughter." Quigg smiled grandly. "You don't realize it, Mr. Wehl, but you're just about to slide back into the Big Power Seat."

"What do you mean?"

"Bernard Rayburn is dying."

"Dying?" He felt a stillness inside him.

"Europa fever. He wants to return the power to you."

"But I'm old, sick," he protested.

"Nothing that can't be cured," Quigg returned. "But first we'll have to work on your memory. That's essential."

"It won't do much good," he said slowly. "I've tried and tried. Nothing comes through except fleeting glimpses that are gone before I really see them."

"Nothing more?"

"Only what I've told you. When I try to think, it's like looking into a black well. There is no light, no form, nothing. It's terrifying."

"What is?"

"The emptiness of the mind." He buried his face in his hands. "Please, I can't think."

Quigg rose and glanced at the doctor. Meador came forward. Grasping Wehl's arm at the wrist, he plunged a needle into the flesh. Wehl tried to jerk free.

"Don't be frightened," Meador said. "It'll help you to sleep."

"But I just woke up," he protested.

"Relax." Meador pulled the needle free.

"You'll feel better when you wake up," Quigg encouraged.

"I don't want to stay here," he cried.

"You won't be here long."

"My daughter!"

"She'll be overjoyed." Quigg smiled reassuringly.

"I . . . don't want to be . . ."

"Sleep," Meador intoned softly.

"Sleep," he murmured. He blinked, wondering why the room was growing dark. Craxton Wehl, he thought, I'm

Craxton Wehl. Now he had a real name, one that was all his own. Mura would be pleased to hear that.

He was drifting, drifting, drifting . . .

Quigg gazed at the drugged patient. "Get inside his mind," he instructed. "Turn it inside out."

Meador arched his eyes. "That's a violation of professional ethics."

"One thousand cpu," he snapped.

"But we do have some flexibility," Meador said quickly. He reached down, lifted Wehl's eyelid, then released it and watched it slide down over the glazed orb. Rolling a small cart alongside the bed, he depilated two spots on the skull and attached a pair of electrodes.

The alpha waves came on, riding slowly across the face of an oscilloscope. They peaked at a steady ten cycles per second. Meador opened the sleeping man's eye again and briefly directed a bright beam into it. The alpha waves took on the frequency of a flickering light. He adjusted a dial and studied the beta and delta waves, the small kappa waves superimposed atop them.

Apparently satisfied with what he found, he injected the patient's arm with another solution. Wehl twitched and groaned. "Have to wait a few moments for it to take effect," Meador said.

"What is it?"

"A chemical to help unlock the memory."

"What was that bit about the fish eye?"

"Oh, that." Meador stroked his jaw. "His view of the universe as distorted symbolizes his own confusion. He can't admit that he's confused, hence attributes it to the outer world."

"But why a fish eye?" Quigg looked puzzled.

"That's fundamental to his own particular type of escape," Meador explained. "He's hoping to start life anew."

"I don't get it."

"He's fled backward in time. By viewing the world as he evidently believes our remote ancestors must have seen it—through bulging eyes adapted to the darkness of the primeval seas—he's expressing his hope of being born anew."

"He believes that?" asked Quigg incredulously.

"Of a certainty." Meador's smile was supercilious.

"What's that bit about the stars being blotted out?"

"His hope of obliterating the present world," Meador said. "Note that he spoke of a gigantic blob. Again that suggests the primeval planet—the past erasing the present."

"That's deep stuff," Quigg admitted. He held a grudging admiration for the other.

"Very deep." Meador turned his attention to the patient. He fiddled with the dials on the instrument cart, then ran a portable electrode slowly across Wehl's forehead, watching the oscilloscope. Small, irregular waves peaked on the screen.

"Can you hear me?" Meador asked.

"Y-yes." The mumbled word came haltingly.

"What's your name?"

"Name?" There was a long silence.

"Can't he remember?" asked Quigg urgently.

Meador shook his head. "He won't accept the fact that he's Craxton Wehl. Wehl was self-centered, an egoist, power-mad. He also was paranoiac, a man caught in the web of his own delusions. That he foisted them off on the outer world made no difference; inwardly he knew what he was. And he knew that he was hated, despised."

"What's that got to do with it?" demanded Quigg.

"He was trying to escape from the man he was." Meador glanced around. "Incidentally, how did he escape from Sundberg's?"

"He teleported."

"My God!"

"That's a Q classification," Quigg admonished.

"Craxton Wehl a teleport? I can't believe it!" Understanding flooded Meador's face. "Is that why you wanted that weird music?"

"To distract him, keep him from concentrating," Quigg acknowledged. "A teleport has to concentrate to make the jump. I got that straight from Sundberg."

Meador shook his head incredulously. "I still can't believe it."

"Nevertheless it's true. Probe him, man. I have to find out what makes him tick."

"Why?" Meador looked uncertain.

"Bernard Rayburn wants to return the power to him. I told you that."

"Then why is he here? Why don't you return him? I don't like probing a man who's apt to become premier again."

"I believe he's the victim of a plot," Quigg exclaimed hoarsely. He had the frantic feeling that Meador was about to withdraw. "I think someone's trying to prevent him from returning to the Big Power Seat. They might even stoop to murder."

"Franckel?" Meador was ashen-faced.

"I wouldn't breathe the name in that connection."

"Franckel would have me on Pluto in no time flat, Quigg."

"If he got the Big Power Seat, yes. We can't allow that, Meador."

"What's that got to do with my probing Wehl?"

"I believe Wehl knows what he's up against. It's there, locked in his memory. If I can discover what it is, I can take steps to protect him. It's a duty that I owe my clients, Meador, and it's your duty."

"I don't like it, Quigg!"

"Two thousand if you open him up like a clamshell!"

"I can't be bought, Quigg."

"Five thousand!"

"I'll try," Meador exclaimed huskily. He turned back to Wehl, asking terse questions while running the electrode around the base of his skull. The small kappa waves jiggled and jumped. Aside from a few incoherent mumblings, the drugged man remained silent.

Quigg demanded impatiently, "Why doesn't he answer?"

"I can't reach his memory banks!"

"He answered when you asked if he could hear you!"

"That doesn't require deep memory, Quigg."

"You've got to reach him!"

"How?" Meador gestured toward the oscilloscope. "Look at that tau wave, Quigg. Flat! The drug should have opened his memory banks—the deep ones buried far down in the cortex. It should have blasted him open, but it didn't. The absence of the tau wave proves that. He can't be probed!"

"Could a peeper reach him?"

64

"My God, do you have one?"

"A partial."

"That's against the law, Quigg. That's Pluto talk!"

"The man's safe. He's worked with me for years."

"He couldn't help, Quigg. Wehl can't be reached either by peeper or drug."

"What do you mean?"

"He's been mindblocked!"

"Good God!" Quigg's hands trembled. "No one would dare!"

"Someone dared, Quigg."

"Murdering a man's mind is worse than murdering his body! You must be mistaken!"

"I'm never mistaken," Meador returned stiffly.

"Sundberg!" Quigg clenched his fists.

"I'm making no accusations," Meador said cautiously.

"It had to be Sundberg! It's a plot, Meador. Sundberg must be working for Franckel."

"For God's sake, don't say that. The walls have ears!"

"Can the block be removed?"

"Where is it, Quigg? In what form?" Meador shrugged helplessly. "Only the person who put it there can remove it."

"If you use drugs, shock therapy, hypnosis . . . ?"

"No use," Meador cut in.

"You can tear his brain apart, bit by bit, cell by cell. If you can't get around the block, rip it away!"

"I'd destroy his brain."

"It's your duty, Meador!"

"No!"

"Ten thousand cpu's?"

"It's impossible, Quigg."

"Can't you bypass the block, short-circuit him?"

"The shock would kill him!"

"Fifteen thousand!"

"I can't violate the medical code, Quigg." Meador shook his head. "I can't risk murder for that price."

"Every man has a price, Meador."

"With honest men it comes high."

"How high?" Quigg demanded hoarsely.

"One hundred thousand plus a ticket to Mars!"

"One hundred thousand?" Quigg was aghast. "By the moons of Jupiter, Meador, the job doesn't pay a tenth of that. I'm doing it as a public service."

"I can't afford that kind of thinking, Quigg."

Damn Sundberg! Quigg gazed helplessly at the drugged man. "Keep him knocked! Keep that music going while I figure something out!"

He rushed from the room, out into the night. His brow felt fevered in the cool air. Mindblock! he thought savagely. The stakes were piling higher and higher and higher. A fortune, and the key was locked in Wehl's mind! He programmed his aircar, switched it to automatic, and viciously jabbed the start button.

The vehicle rose swiftly, climbing toward the stars.

SEVEN

Sundberg had klotched him!

Quigg cursed savagely. If Sundberg had lied about the amnesia, what else had he lied about? The teleportation angle? More to the point, why had he lied? That information would be worth a goodly fortune. And the secret was there, locked in Wehl's mind!

He forced himself to think more calmly. Sundberg was treading a dangerous path. To impose a mindblock was to risk Pluto; to mindblock a former premier was all but unthinkable. Yet Sundberg had done just that. Why?

His excitement quickened. Sundberg would never have risked such a step without ample protection. From high up, he amended. Bernard Rayburn? If so, why did Rayburn want Wehl mindblocked? Was it possible the succession ceremony never had occurred? The idea staggered him. If that were so, Rayburn's alleged Europa fever could be an elaborate smokescreen to cover the real reason for the frantic attempt to get Wehl back. If Sundberg succeeded, exit Mr. Wehl, he thought cynically.

But that didn't explain the teleportation, if that's how Wehl escaped. Neither did it explain why Wehl hadn't died in surgery—the logical step if Wehl posed some sort of threat. Oh, it didn't explain a lot of things.

Another possibility was Franckel. Could Franckel be the power behind Sundberg's act? He shook his head irritably. If Rayburn were dying, Franckel wouldn't have had Wehl mindblocked; he would have had him assassinated. All in all, none of it made much sense.

He felt irritated at what he didn't know. But one thing was certain: the stakes were enormous. Somehow they revolved around the secret in Wehl's mind. Sundberg would know the truth, and possibly his staff. At least they'd know about the mindblock. He had the distinct conviction that none of them would talk.

Would Madelyn Wehl know the real story? Not if her father were the victim. But neither did it seem likely that any great conspiracy could swirl so closely by her without her having some inkling of something amiss. She was too power-conscious for that. One other thing was certain: she'd pay a goodly sum to have him returned safely, especially if he were coming back to resume the power. That would send her own balloon soaring.

A chime signaled the approach to his destination. Peering through the windshield, he saw the tall, white tower in which he maintained his offices. In the late hour, most of the windows were dark. He switched to manual control, dropped from the traffic lane, and homed in on the rooftop landing pad. Parking the car, he rode the elevator to his private suite.

As he opened the door, an alarm clamored in his brain; the hair at the base of his skull prickled. He froze, staring into the darkened rooms. The dim glow through the windows revealed nothing. His imagination?

He forced himself to cross the short space to his office and flick on the light. A dark, surly-faced man with deep-set eyes and a white slash across one cheek was watching him bemusedly from behind his own desk.

Quigg recoiled, visibly shaken. "Who are you?" he demanded.

"A possible client."

"How did you get in here?"

"It wasn't difficult."

"The office is closed," Quigg stated. He noticed how the scar pulled one corner of the mouth slightly awry. "If you have business, make an appointment with my secretary."

"The office is open," the other replied tolerantly. "Sit down."

"You've seen my ad? No job under fifty thousand cpu's."

"Sit down," the other repeated coldly.

"If you would be good enough to vacate my desk."

"My pleasure." The scar-faced man rose indolently and plopped down in a comfortable chair against the wall.

Quigg sat. "I don't do business with clients whose names I don't know," he said stiffly.

"You will this time."

"What's your proposition?"

"I want Craxton Wehl."

Quigg suppressed a quick fright. "Sorry, not interested." He dropped a hand, pressing two buttons at the side of his desk. One activated a tape recorder; the other started a hidden camera.

"You'd better be."

"Are you threatening me?"

"You could put it that way."

"Try my competitors," Quigg snapped. "They might be interested but I'm not. Craxton Wehl is dynamite."

"Then why'd you grab him?"

"Who told you that?" He fought his dismay.

"Such things are my business."

Quigg's eyes narrowed. "That knowledge could be dangerous."

"Perhaps to you, not to me."

He forced himself to relax. "I already have a client. Ethics won't permit me to serve two different parties on the same case."

"Ethics," the other sneered. "You can solve that dilemma by dropping the other client."

"Keep talking," Quigg instructed.

"How much is Sundberg paying you?"

"That's confidential."

"I'll double the offer."

"I doubt that you would if you knew the price."

"How much?"

"Two hundred thousand fixed fee," Quigg replied coolly. When the other didn't blink, he added, "Plus a fifty percent bonus for successful performance."

"Agreed."

68

"I was quoting my terms with Sundberg," he said.

"I'll double the fixed fee. The bonus stands."

Quigg shook his head. "Sundberg could sue me for breach of contract, strip me to the bone. I can't risk it."

"My client will assume any damages."

"Who is your client?"

"None of your damned business, Quigg."

His first nervousness past, Quigg took the time to consider the offer. A man who didn't blink at a price tag of four hundred thousand with a fifty percent bonus for successful completion clearly represented wealth and power, or both. Bernard Rayburn? That was possible but he didn't believe so; Rayburn would have assigned the job to Jing Lee Hom. No doubt the agent was working on it now.

Franckel? That was more probable. But Wehl's only use to Franckel would be as a dead man. If Wehl were worth that much to Franckel, what might he be worth to Madelyn Wehl, especially if she knew that Franckel was bidding for her father? Careful, he cautioned himself, you're looking at Pluto. Nevertheless, he felt his excitement mount.

"Well?" the scar-faced man demanded.

"I'll have to consider it."

"Don't try to cross me, Quigg."

"Cross you?" He arched his eyes. "We have no agreement."

"We will have!"

He said decisively, "Try me tomorrow night, same time."

"While you try to sell to someone else?"

"Please." He looked pained.

"If you're planning that, forget it." The scar-faced man tapped his jacket significantly. Quigg's eyes didn't miss the bulge.

"I won't be threatened," he said coldly.

"You just have been." The scar-faced man rose.

"Wait," Quigg implored. His jaw muscles worked convulsively. "Honest men trust each other. Is your client Franckel? I'll respect your confidence."

"You won't have the opportunity, Quigg." Laughing nastily, he left the room. Quigg snapped off the automatic camera and tape recorder. He'd known soon enough who his visitor had been; the photos should make the identification simple. He'd be very much surprised if the other didn't prove to be an agent for Franckel.

He sat back slowly. Franckel was gambling for big stakes—far too big to allow such a small matter as murder stand in his way. Bernard Rayburn was dying and the Big Power Seat would be left open if something happened to Craxton Wehl—that was the size of it. He had small doubt but that the scar-faced man's job was to see that something did happen to Wehl.

He felt uneasy. Klotching Sundberg was one thing; trying to klotch Franckel was something quite different. Franckel already had challenged Rayburn's right to office. Had he also masterminded the theft of Rayburn's birth certificate from the public records? Probably, but that was peanuts. What counted was that Franckel wouldn't stop this side of murder. Worse, his recent visitor knew of his deal with Sundberg—that he had snatched Wehl!

His brow suddenly felt sweaty. Not that he'd admitted anything, he told himself. Neither had he committed himself. At the same time, he'd left the door open for future negotiations. He'd handled the situation quite nicely, he thought. But he'd have to work fast.

He placed a call to Meador. When the doctor's face came on the screen, he said urgently, "I want a guard placed outside Wehl's door. No one is to enter except you or the nurse. And keep that music going."

"What's wrong?" Meador demanded worriedly.

"Just a precaution." He broke the connection before the medic could answer, then leaned back to consider his next move. If Madelyn Wehl was ready to shake the money tree—really shake it—he'd unload the old man on her before another day was past. Then, perhaps, it would be worth something to Franckel's man to know Wehl's whereabouts.

He rubbed his hands briskly at the prospect.

In the outer corridor, the scar-faced man removed a suction microphone from the wall, dropped it into his pocket, and strolled toward the elevator.

Quigg dropped the aircar from the coastal traffic stream and swung eastward into the rising sun. Whipping past below were the stately mansions of the Malibu hills.

Enclosed behind high electric fences with guard towers along their perimeters, these were homes of the high and mighty.

He eyed the scene covetously. But if his deal with Madelyn Wehl proved successful ... He shot a sidelong glance at Obie Frye's thin figure, slouched in the seat beside him. The peeper's narrow face reflected the worry he'd felt since he'd learned the true identity of the man who'd called himself Gerald Sundberg.

Quigg's lip curled disdainfully. Despite his talent, the peeper lived at the bottom of the human pool; power frightened him. He's a fool, Quigg thought. He'd never learned that the only real power was that backed by the charge plate. If Frye wouldn't use his talent, he'd use it for him. Properly directed, the peeper could pay off handsomely. But right now his job was to keep his presence of mind long enough to read Madelyn Wehl's thoughts.

Frye stirred restlessly.

"Remember to keep your mouth shut," Quigg warned. "Don't say a thing unless she asks."

"Won't she wonder why you brought me?" he asked nervously.

"I'll take care of that." Quigg stared ahead, his anticipation tinged with unease. He'd gotten the appointment with Madelyn Wehl quickly enough when he'd stated his business, or what little of it he'd chosen to reveal. Yet his uneasiness persisted.

Had it to do with Wehl's mindblock? Or was it what lay behind the mindblock? Examining the questions, he felt his bafflement grow. He had the feeling of having discovered the door to a treasure trove only to find it locked. And the big power winds were blowing; a thousand tornadoes danced around him.

How did the scar-faced man fit into the picture? Remembering his visitor's implied threat, he shivered. Certainly the man was Franckel's agent. Was Franckel preparing a power grab? Or was it something else? Whatever the true situation, Craxton Wehl represented a considerable fortune. *If he played it right!* The fear that he might not made him wince.

Far ahead, perched on an upland meadow that gave it splendid isolation, Wehl House wheeled toward him. A spacious greensward, dotted with graceful elm and eu-

71

calyptus, held the quietness of a painting. A traffic tower off to one side marked the landing pad.

Two armed aircars swooped down from the sky, bracketing him. His radio crackled to life. "You are in private airspace," a voice blared. "Identify!"

Quigg stated his name and business and received instructions to land. The aircars followed him down. Parked, he opened the door and stepped out. A guard stalked toward him from the tower.

"Your identity?" he snapped. Quigg produced a card. The guard scanned it briefly and murmured into a wrist radio, listening for an answer. When it came, he directed Quigg to follow him.

"I brought my assistant." Quigg motioned Frye to accompany him and followed the guard. The peeper glanced furtively around the opulent room into which they were escorted. Quigg smiled condescendingly. Such richness as this lay in his own future.

Madelyn Wehl descended a gilded staircase to meet them. Blonde and stately, she would have been beautiful were it not for the hardness of her features. Quigg had the impression they had been molded in a quick-freeze. But the pale blue eyes, the narrow bridge of the nose, and the set of the jaw—a certain tightness around the mouth—undeniably were Wehl's. There was no contesting the fact that this was the old man's daughter.

Her eyes dismissed Frye with a glance, settling on Quigg. "Be seated," she said coldly.

Quigg motioned the peeper to a chair and sat. "It was good of you to give me your time."

"What do you know of my father?"

"There are rumors, Miss Wehl." He attempted a smile. "In my business we listen for such things."

"What rumors?"

"He has been seen here and there, Miss Wehl. After all, he is the best-known man in the Solar Empire."

"Who has seen him?" she demanded.

"I can't answer that, Miss Wehl."

"Why not?"

Quigg said carefully, "I have another party interested in the same information."

"Sundberg, I know." She tossed her head.

72

"I don't regard my contract with Sundberg as firm," he replied quickly. "I was referring to a third party."

"Franckel?"

"It wouldn't be ethical to give that information."

"You're shopping for a buyer." Her voice was ice.

"That's a crass way to put it but, yes, I work for fees," he admitted.

"How much?"

"There are some unusual circumstances that would make the job quite expensive," he countered.

"What circumstances?"

"The teleportation bit."

"Ridiculous!" she snapped. "He even hates aircars."

"Nevertheless, he teleported." He took the time to study her. "If the story is false, why did Sundberg retain me to find him?"

"I can't answer that."

"Can't or won't?"

"Can't," she said. "How much?"

"Seven hundred thousand fixed fee plus a fifty percent bonus for delivering your father here by sunset tomorrow," he said boldly.

"Is that a guarantee?"

"We never fail—our ad states that quite clearly."

"My secretary will make the arrangements." With a disdainful glance, she rose and turned toward the staircase. He glowed inwardly. Seven hundred thousand with a fifty percent bonus, all set for signing and sealing. Could he do better with Franckel's man? Perhaps, but this was money in the hand. He brushed aside a momentary regret that he hadn't named a higher figure. A rustle brought him around; it was Madelyn Wehl's secretary.

Business completed, they were escorted back to the aircar. As it lifted from the pad, Quigg asked anxiously, "What was she thinking?"

"I didn't get much of a chance to peep her," Frye answered uneasily.

"You must have gotten something," he snapped.

"She was wondering how much you knew."

"Plenty!" Quigg smiled with self-satisfaction. "What else?"

"She was worried."

"About her father?"

73

"Death." The peeper glanced covertly at him. "The premier is dying."

"So, it's true!" He suppressed a quick surprise. Somehow he had always doubted that story. Rayburn appeared too strong, too healthy—the Europa fever too coincidental. Sundberg had been quite testy on that point. But he *was* dying! Obie Frye had plucked that neatly from Madelyn Wehl's mind.

"Is that true?" Frye asked timidly.

"Shut up, let me think," he barked. He felt suddenly edgy. If Rayburn were dying, then Sundberg's story well could be true. Rayburn would need Wehl to fill the Big Power Seat before Franckel or one of the other governors could seize it. Given that situation, Franckel would move heaven and hell to eliminate Wehl. That would account for the scar-faced man's interest in the former premier; his business was assassination.

If the scar-faced man represented Franckel! But did he? That assumption lay in the realm of pure guess. Yet it all added up, except for one thing: Why had Craxton Wehl been mindblocked?

He cursed savagely. That last item pulled the foundation right out from under the whole pattern of logic. That and the teleport bit. If Wehl were a teleport, his daughter certainly hadn't been aware of it. Or, as Sundberg had suggested, could the capability have resulted from the operation?

The mindblock was the problem. Who had ordered it, and why? What great secret did it conceal? If he knew that, the seven hundred thousand might appear like peanuts, he reflected bitterly. Perhaps he should have doubled the sum, or tripled it. Madelyn Wehl had called him a shopper. Well, he still had time to shop. He smiled grimly as he wove the aircar into the coastal traffic pattern.

When he reached his office, his secretary handed him an envelope. "The identification you ordered on the photographs," she reminded him.

"Oh!" He retreated to his office and gingerly opened it. Spilling the contents on his desk, he stared for a long moment at the lean visage of the scar-faced man before lifting the accompanying report.

Major Leon Sobel, Empire Intelligence, chief aide to

Colonel Jing Lee Hom—his fingers trembled as he read the brief words. The scar-faced man worked for Hom! He groped to assimilate the significance of it. Sobel could be playing a double game; so could Hom. Or were they playing it straight, attempting to get Wehl back to assume the power?

He shook his head in disbelief. No one played it straight, not with the stakes what they were. It seemed quite likely that Jing Lee Hom, seeing the handwriting on the wall, had thrown in his lot with Franckel to preserve his own power after Rayburn died. How better could he do it than by murdering Wehl?

But the facts weren't as important as the implications. Franckel could have him assassinated in a second. So could Rayburn, or Wehl, if he was returned to power. And if he crossed Jing Lee Hom, he was worse than dead. Empire Intelligence paid lip service to the due process of law, but that was all.

I'm getting jittery, he reflected. He hadn't done anything to warrant assassination—neither to Franckel nor Rayburn nor Wehl. Everything considered, his best course was to return Wehl safely to his daughter. When Wehl's memory was restored, would it extend back to his interrogation in Meador's sanitarium? Meador had assured him that it wouldn't.

He chewed his lip vexedly. The wind in the money tree was weakening, but better a barren money tree than Pluto, or death. He'd turn Wehl over to his daughter, collect the seven hundred thousand plus the bonus, and call it quits. Perhaps he could safely guard himself by reporting the transaction to Hom. He sighed wistfully.

Tomorrow was another day.

EIGHT

"Aaaugh!"
The fish eye! The black, distorted sky! The blob that . . .

75

"One, two, three, four . . ."
Sundberg's pale face under the surgical lights . . .
"Listen, listen, listen, listen . . ."
Wehl House set on the greensward, the eucalyptus . . .
Clang! Clang! Clang!
Mr. Krant's candy shop and . . .
A horn blaring . . .
Mura's room, Mura's room, Mura's room . . .
"Shut off that damned noise!"

He awoke, trembling, drenched with sweat, the scream on his lips. A guitar twanged. He threw his hands to his face, shuddering. God, where am I?

"One, two, three, four . . ."

"Shut it off!" he screamed. He tore his hands from his eyes, staring at the white walls and ceiling, then he remembered. Wehl! He was Craxton Wehl, the former premier! Little motes of memory flitted across the horizons of his mind. He was Craxton Wehl, had been ill, had vanished from Sundberg's clinic. Craxton Wehl, former premier—that was incredible!

Felix Quigg! He remembered now—Quigg had been retained to . . . His daughter! He had a daughter! Quigg had . . .

"One, two, three, four . . ."

He started to scream again, then clamped his lips shut, grasping at the memories before they fled. They'd been trying to probe him! Narcohypnosis, that was it! The man called Meador had stabbed him with a needle! Fragmentary recollections danced in his mind. Lying there, drugged, he had been conscious of words and snatches of conversation that . . .

Teleport! Stunned, he gazed upward at the ceiling. He had teleported from Sundberg's clinic! He could all but hear Quigg's nasal voice as the words came back. Utterly fantastic.

"One, two, three, four . . ."

Meador had said . . .

"Listen, listen, listen, listen . . ."

Mindblock! The word crashed into his consciousness. He had been mindblocked; he clearly remembered that. He groaned. What was true and what was fantasy? It all seemed a hellish nightmare.

The guitar twanged.

The horn blared.

He attempted to close his ears to the cacophony of sound and force himself to calmness. If only he could capture the dim memories that hovered just beyond his grasp. Perhaps it wasn't all a mad dream. The teleportation would explain his escape from jail, his magical reappearance in Mura's apartment.

Why her apartment? The struggle to remember brought strange feelings of unreality; visual fragments floated eerily through his mind. Glade Avenue, the tower at the space terminal, Mr. Krant's candy store, the distorted sky—they all danced crazily in his brain.

Mindblock!

The word thundered back, staggering him with its import. He had been cut off from his past; all the long years of his life had been torn from him, sealed off in some unreachable part of his brain. Why? In what strange fantasy was he trapped? Craxton Wehl, former premier, the mindblocked teleport! He laughed harshly. Being Gerald Sundberg had been far simpler.

He struggled . . .

"One, two, three, four . . ."

to bring his thoughts into order. Quigg was lying, that was evident. Had he been retained . . .

"Listen, listen, listen, listen . . ."

to return him to his daughter—or was it to Sundberg's clinic?—he would have done so. Instead, he had brought him here, had subjected him to narcohypnosis, had attempted to burrow into his mind. What had Quigg been after?

The guitar twanged.

He threw up his hands to shut out the shrill sound that came with the sharpness of a needle. Bits and pieces and fragments of memory danced, collided, coalesced, splintered—darted to and fro like fireflies in the night of his skull.

Was he really Craxton Wehl, as Quigg had claimed, or was he Gerald Sundberg? (*My God, that horn!*) Sundberg . . . He ran the name slowly through his mind and was

77

rewarded with the vague recollection of a clinic. Not this clinic, he knew; its geometry was all wrong.

Sundberg and . . . a nurse! Nurse Caldwell! Her name inexplicably flooded back. There had been an attendant called Kelsey! He trembled with excitement.

Sundberg . . . He tested the name again, his concentration on the wispy images that leaped like small gray ghosts in the shadowy corridors of his mind. A small cubicle took form, its walls white and gleaming; a surgical light shone down. A narrow face with a high forehead, the skin shiny under the hairline, moved into his field of vision. Close-set dark eyes peered down at him from above a gauze mask.

Sundberg! My God, there was Sundberg! The knowledge screamed inside him. Then he couldn't be Gerald Sundberg! He had to be . . . Craxton Wehl!

"One, two, three, four . . ."

He was Craxton Wehl, former premier!

"Listen, listen, listen, listen . . ."

Craxton Wehl, the mindblocked teleport!

The guitar twanged.

The horn blared.

"Shut it off!" he screamed. Fighting savagely, he pushed against the straps that held him to the bed. "Shut it off! Shut it off!" the words ended in a strangled sob. No use, no use.

He fell back panting, determined to retain his grip on this new-formed reality. He was Craxton Wehl! He was! He was! He was Craxton Wehl and no one could take that away from him! He had a name and he had an identity that was all his own! A sobbing laugh escaped his lips; dying away, it left him staring at the white ceiling.

"Am I Craxton Wehl?" He murmured the question apprehensively. Why would Quigg lie about a thing like that? He must be Craxton Wehl. But if so, why was he here, strapped down like a common prisoner? What had Quigg been trying to dredge from the depths of his mind?

Teleport! The word leaped back. He could teleport, escape! Was that possible? The thought jolted him. How did a teleport teleport? It had something to do with concentration; he remembered that much. Concentration and destination. But how could he concentrate with that crazy music?

The music! Of course, that was it—the music was

intended to keep him from concentrating. The music and that raucous voice! They couldn't stop him. He pressed his hands to his ears to close out the sound.

"One, two, three, four . . ."

The words came faintly as if from a distance. Sundberg's clinic! He struggled to resurrect it in his mind. If he could get there he could force the medic to tell him the truth. Nebulous outlines took form; they wavered and danced at the periphery of reality.

"Listen, listen, listen, listen . . ."

"Don't listen," he told himself fiercely. Think! Concentrate! There's a doctor named Sundberg, a clinic in the sky. *In the sky?* Yes, in the sky! The House of Hope—he remembered now. He had the sudden illusion that he was no longer in the room, but was in the black night of space.

The stars screamed down!

He was lying on a table in the white-walled room; a cone of light shone down. Sundberg, the lower part of his face masked, watched him through dark, intent eyes. The nurse hovered at his side. There was . . .

Danger! The word shrieked in his brain. He jerked back to awareness, caught with terror. His nerves sang like taut wires in a high wind. The sweat sprang to his palms. *Danger! Danger! The alarm grew to a wild clamor in his skull.*

He jerked his gaze toward the door; the danger lay just beyond it! How had he sensed that? *I have to teleport,* he thought desperately. Sundberg's clinic. He caught his breath as the door opened and a swarthy man stepped quickly inside, lugging an inert body. Kicking the door shut behind him, he dropped the body to the floor. Horrified, Wehl recognized it as that of a private guard. The half-open mouth and glazed eyes told him the man was dead.

He looked fearfully at the newcomer—the dark, hard face, the slashing scar across the cheek that pulled one corner of the mouth slightly awry. "Who are you?" he gasped.

"The knowledge won't do you much good, Wehl."

"You killed him," he accused.

"He's dead, all right." The scar-faced man cocked his head as a horn blared. "That music makes a good screen."

"What do you mean?"

"Just an observation." He looked contemptuously at the body. "He was keeping you prisoner."

"I know." Wehl's jaws worked convulsively.

"Why?"

"I don't know." Wehl regarded him steadily. "What's your interest?"

"We haven't time for that. Did Quigg and that medic question you?"

"They put me under narcohypnosis," he admitted.

"Don't you remember anything?"

"Not much." He smiled wanly.

"You know who you are," the other reminded pointedly.

"Quigg told me."

"Did he say what he was after?"

"He said I'd suffered amnesia, had escaped from a clinic. He said he'd been retained to find me."

"Did he say who retained him?"

"My daughter. I have a daughter, you know. Her name is Madelyn."

"What else did he say?"

"That I had passed the power to a man named Bernard Rayburn."

"Anything else?"

"Nothing." He shook his head defeatedly. "But I learned something while I was under the drug. Their words came through."

"Learned what?"

"Quigg said I was a teleport."

"Oh, that." The scar-faced man's eyes sharpened. "Are you?"

"Is such a thing possible?"

"It happens, Wehl."

"That's difficult to believe," he murmured. He raised his gaze to the scarred face. "The doctor said I was mindblocked."

"Mindblocked?" The other was startled.

He nodded vigorously. "That's what he told Quigg."

"Quigg didn't know?"

"He seemed quite shocked. He tried to get Meador—that's the doctor—to break it. Meador said it was impossible."

"Mindblocked!" The scar-faced man stroked his jaw. "I'll have to think about that."

"What do you mean?"

"Do you remember actually passing the power to Bernard Rayburn?"

He shook his head.

"Perhaps Rayburn pulled a coup, eh?"

"Tricked me?"

"It's conceivable. That opens interesting possibilities."

"What are you thinking?" he cried.

"You might still be premier. Perhaps that was the reason for the mindblock—to make you forget that the ceremony never occurred."

"Would they dare such a thing?"

"A lot of people don't like you, Wehl. You were ready to be toppled. Then a smart politician like Rayburn comes along . . ." The scar-faced man smiled bleakly. "If true, that information is worth a tidy fortune."

"Did you come to help me escape?"

"No." The other's eyes grew wintry.

"Why did you come?" he whispered hoarsely. A terrible premonition gripped him. The man had killed the guard in cold blood. He was mad! He had to get out of here. He had to teleport, teleport, teleport.

"To kill you."

"Why?" He tried to keep the fright from his voice.

"To keep you from returning to the Big Power Seat."

"Why would I return? Rayburn has it; you said that yourself."

"Rayburn's dying."

"Oh!" He remembered Quigg's words. "Is it true?"

"Europa fever, or so he claims. He wants to return the power to keep it from falling into Franckel's hands."

"Franckel, I remember that name."

"You should," the scar-faced man said tonelessly.

"But if the succession ceremony never took place, as you appear to believe, why would he want to return the power to me? That doesn't make sense."

"In that event it would make sense to lure you back, kill you, make certain you were out of the way."

"Why would he do a thing like that?" Wehl's head jerked up. "If you believe that's true, what do you gain by killing me? Rayburn still will have the power."

81

"That's a surmise, Wehl. I can't take the chance that he might be telling the truth."

"About dying?" Wehl stared into the glittering black eyes. "But suppose he's not?"

"You ask too many questions, Wehl."

"You can't . . . just murder me," he whispered hoarsely.

"No?" The scar-faced man gave a terrible smile. "Murder is my business."

"No!" The denial exploded from his lips. Sundberg's clinic! He had to escape! He fought to resurrect it in his mind, recapture the small room with the white walls, white ceiling. The image flickered in his consciousness, receded, came back stronger. He had to teleport, teleport, teleport.

"The world won't miss you, Wehl." The words came from far away.

The horn blared.

"No!" he shouted again. He had to teleport, teleport, teleport. He had . . .

The scar-faced man's hand came from a pocket holding a blaster. He lifted it, then let it drop; his jaw went slack.

He was staring at an empty bed.

The silence was a thunder in his ears.

His eyes snapped open and he rolled over on the hard floor, gazing at the white walls that enclosed him. Illuminated only by the dim glow through a partially open door, they appeared forbiddingly austere.

The music had stopped! With the realization came the memory of the scar-faced man. He shuddered as he pushed himself to a sitting position and looked around. The sole furnishing was a small cot. The scar-faced man was gone!

It wasn't the same room! A sudden stillness gripped him. This room was smaller, more barren. He struggled with his thoughts. The scar-faced man had come to kill him: *"To keep you from returning to the Big Power Seat,"* he'd said. He had pulled a blaster from his pocket and . . .

That was all; his memory ended there. Now he was here, in a small cubicle. It was the same as when he'd vanished from jail, only to reappear in Mura's apartment. There had been oblivion, a transition, a reemergence.

Sundberg's clinic! Suddenly he understood. He had escaped, had teleported! The knowledge left him awed. Was he mad, deluded? The strange walls enclosing him told him he was not. Somehow he had transcended time and space, or at least space. Then what Quigg told him must be true: he was Craxton Wehl!

He passed a hand wearily over his face. Craxton Wehl, the former premier—he had passed the power to Bernard Rayburn, had been mindblocked, had escaped. That was fantastic. But was it true? When he looked into his mind he saw only a wild, disorganized, bizarre thing, filled with fragments of nightmares. It was like a scene from hell in which bats flitted through eerie caverns lighted by the dancing flames from below.

Was he Craxton Wehl? He forced his attention to the question. Had he passed the power to Bernard Rayburn, or had Bernard Rayburn robbed him of it? The latter might explain the mindblock; it also might explain the attempt to kill him: Rayburn wanted him out of the way. But it didn't explain everything. Yet he was mindblocked, and he could teleport. That much, at least, was true.

Quigg wanted to pillage his mind; the scar-faced man wanted to murder him; Rayburn wanted to give him back the power. None of that made sense. Only Mura made sense, he thought. She was the only real person of the lot. The rest were phantoms come to plague him.

Aware of the absolute silence, he rose and peered out through the partially open door. The strange geometry of the construction momentarily puzzled him until he remembered that he was speeding through space in a satellite. Had Quigg told him that, or had it come from some deeper well? The knowledge that he had teleported to a satellite brought a shiver.

He studied the empty corridor apprehensively. The doors to the other cubicles were closed. The nurse's room, Sundberg's office and private quarters at the far end—the details flooded his mind. He resurrected the locations of the attendant's room, the galley, the maintenance on the lower deck, the surgery almost across from him. The lander wells were just beyond.

For an instant he had the impression of standing in front of Mura's apartment, gazing along Glade Avenue. There was the same sense of familiarity, the same sense of recognition, yet with no real sense of reality. Yet this *was* reality; he knew it beyond a doubt.

Faint, flickering pictures tumbled through his consciousness. It was, he thought, as if someone were shaking his brain, stirring the images. Nurse Caldwell, the attendant Kelsey, Doctor Gerald Sundberg—their faces floated through his mind's eye. A tall, blond giant strode toward him, the eyes tawny in the lean face. Bernard Rayburn! Wehl recoiled and the vision vanished. The place is spooked, he thought; it was filled with visions from the past.

He stared along the empty corridor, trying to resurrect the image. The tawny face came again; it waxed and waned, danced in his mind, but without the previous clarity. Still it brought a deep sense of recognition. Why was that? It left him with the odd feeling of having viewed a ghost. His heart thumped, a hollow sound.

A sense of urgency swept him. If he could gain access to Sundberg's records, perhaps he could find some clue to what had happened to him, and why. Not that Sundberg would commit such a thing to paper. But he had to try.

Where was everyone? He scanned the empty corridor anew. The nurse was asleep in her room. He jerked violently. How had he known that? The question came with the smash of a fist. But it was true, she was asleep; he knew it with absolute certainty.

He swung his gaze to the attendant's room. Kelsey: memory of the name brought a fleeting impression of a square brown face, unruly hair. A big fellow, good-natured, not too bright—the knowledge flooded back.

Kelsey was ... reading! Startled, he suppressed the exclamation about to burst from his lips. Lord, did his mind reach out, touch theirs? That would be a form of telepathy! Or was it clairvoyance? That's idiotic, he thought. A teleport, yes, but that didn't make him God.

He riveted his attention on Sundberg's door. This time he had no impressions whatever. Perhaps Sundberg wasn't aboard. He stepped into the corridor. Discovery that one of the lander wells was empty brought a surge of hope. Moving softly to the doctor's quarters, he turned the knob and entered. Sundberg was gone! He felt a quick relief.

A search of the desk drawers and cupboards yielded nothing that pertained to him. A steel wall safe caught his eye. He regarded it musingly. Any papers of importance undoubtedly would be locked inside. The speculation disheartened him.

Sundberg's private quarters consisted of a small bedroom with an adjoining bath. One wall was lined with books; another held a niche filled with clothes. A porthole looked out into the vastness of the universe. Through it he saw the sweep of stars.

The neat array of garments in the closet drew his attention. Crylon trousers and jackets from Eurasio, molded weaves from York, colorful capes that but recently had come into vogue—they held a sartorial splendor he couldn't resist.

He selected a pair of pale green trousers, a tan jacket, and an olive-colored cape. Shoes, elegantly handcrafted from genuine synthetic leather, fitted quite nicely. Dressed, he surveyed himself in the mirror. Were it not for his scraggly gray beard, he'd look a good ten years younger—not a day over sixty-five, he reflected.

A small chest caught his eye. He rummaged through it, found a stun gun, and dropped it into his pocket. The feel of the weapon brought a sense of security. He glanced around uncertainly. He'd found nothing that told him anything. All at once he desperately wanted to be back with Mura. This time, he thought proudly, he'd return with a name—one that was all his own.

Suppose he couldn't teleport at will? The thought made him jittery. But he could; he'd proved it. Concentration plus destination—that was the key. That and the magic trigger that lay somewhere in his brain.

He went to the door and peered out into the corridor. The silence reassured him. For a moment he absorbed the clinic's architecture, fixing it in mind for future use, then started toward the cubicle which he'd come to regard as his own.

As he passed the attendant's room, a buzzer sounded to warn of an approaching lander. Frightened, he darted through the nearest door. A glance disclosed a hospital bed, a chair—nothing else. He peered back into the corridor, saw a green light blinking above one of the lander wells. Struggling into a white jacket, Kelsey popped into view.

Sundberg stepped out from the lander well. His thin

85

face appeared harsh and tired. "The premier could be coming up at any time," he snapped. "Prepare his quarters."

"Yes, sir."

Wehl was horrified to see the attendant start toward him. He looked wildly around for a place to hide. Kelsey's square figure loomed in the doorway; an instant later the room was flooded with light.

The attendant stared open-mouthed at him, then swung back into the corridor. "Doctor, doctor!" he shouted. "Patient Seventeen-L is back!"

"Where?" Sundberg screamed shrilly.

"Room C, the one we . . ."

"Get a narco needle, quick!"

Wehl heard footsteps pound toward him. He leaped forward, slammed the door just as a body crashed against it. He gripped the knob to prevent it from being turned, closed his eyes, and tried to concentrate on Mura's apartment.

"Open up!" Sundberg's voice, tinged with panic, came through the thin partition.

"Go away," he shouted hoarsely. He discovered a latch, turned it, and stepped back. I've got to teleport, he thought desperately. The doctor rattled the door.

"Mr. Wehl?" His voice suddenly was conciliatory. Wehl didn't answer. Mura's, he had to get to Mura's. He was dimly aware of Kelsey's footsteps returning.

"Break it down!" Sundberg's order came with a snarl. Someone hammered at the door. Wehl closed his ears to it. I've got to teleport, teleport, teleport. Visions of Mura's apartment danced in his mind. The hammering against the door became more remote.

Mura! Mura!

He was shouting the name in his mind when he vanished.

NINE

Wehl's eyes blinked open.

Mura Breen, her face taut and frightened, was staring down at him. He struggled to a sitting position, aware of the ache in his arms and shoulders. His body felt drained.

"How did you get here?" she whispered.

"I was caught, taken to a sanitarium. Someone tried to kill me."

"Kill you?" She stepped back, startled.

"A scar-faced man. I escaped to Sundberg's clinic."

"I must be crazy."

"No, no," he said hastily. "It's all quite logical."

"Logical?" She gazed disbelievingly at him. "Sundberg's clinic is a satellite. How could you have gotten there?"

He licked his lips drily and whispered, "I teleported."

"Teleported?" She recoiled another step.

"Please, don't be frightened," he urged.

She tried a smile. "I'm trying not to be."

"It's the truth," he said. "I'm a teleport."

"That's how you ... got here?" Some of the disbelief fled from her face, replaced with wonder. "But there are only a dozen, a score at most in the entire empire."

"I ... don't know."

"But all the teleports are known," she whispered. "They're all registered. It's the law."

"Perhaps." His eyes went slowly to her face. "I found out something else about myself. I've been mindblocked."

"Oh, that's terrible!"

"And I know who I am."

"You know?"

He nodded reluctantly. "I'm Craxton Wehl."

"The former premier?" she gasped incredulously.

He nodded.

"I don't believe it!"

"It's the truth," he mumbled.

87

"It can't be. Someone is playing a monstrous joke on you."

"Why can't it be?" he asked testily. "I have to be someone."

"Not Craxton Wehl," she cried. "He was mean, power-mad, a tyrant. They say he went mad!"

"I don't feel that way."

"Oh, you're kind and gentle."

"Perhaps he wasn't all those things," he remonstrated. "Perhaps it was just talk."

"But it wasn't," she insisted. "Did you know he limited the supplies coming to Mars to keep us subservient? He did to all the OutSat worlds. He was afraid to let us grow, advance. His secret police infiltrated our domes. Every strong leader we ever had died in some strange accident or other. Oh, it was Craxton Wehl, all right. So you see, you couldn't be him."

"But I am."

"Oh!" She threw her hands to her face.

"I'm not mean or power-mad," he denied.

"Of course you're not!"

"Yet I'm Craxton Wehl."

"Something is terribly wrong."

"But what?"

"I don't know." She dropped her hands, gazed at him. "You . . . look like him. I said at first you looked familiar."

"I remember."

"But who would believe it? Oh, I'm all mixed up."

"Don't be," he pleaded.

"How did you learn who you were?"

"From Felix Quigg." He told her of what had happened since last he had left her apartment, and how he had willed himself to teleport to and from Sundberg's clinic. As he spoke, she appeared to regain her composure.

When he finished, she asked, "With Bernard Rayburn dying, why did they mindblock you?"

"If he's dying," he corrected. "I don't know that he is; but I do know I'm mindblocked. It had to be Sundberg."

"And that other man, Quigg, what was he after?"

"Whatever might be of value," he answered drily.

"And that scar-faced man—why would be try to kill you?"

"To keep me from returning to power. He said that."

"Then he must be working for someone who's trying to get the power," she declared.

"That makes sense."

"But it still doesn't explain the mindblock."

"I'll find the reason," he promised. He added reluctantly, "I think I might be telepathic."

"Oh!"

"Not that I can read minds," he added hurriedly. "It's more a sense of impressions." He told her how he'd sensed that the nurse was sleeping, that Kelsey was reading, that Sundberg's office was deserted.

She moistened her lips edgily. "That's not exactly telepathy, is it?"

"Not in the usual sense." He considered it. "The impressions come in the form of images, so perhaps it's clairvoyance. But it has to be one or the other; how else could I have known?"

"It's not so shocking—not if you can teleport." Her face grew still. "Isn't that frightening?"

"The ability to teleport? It came as a shock, but the human mind's quite adaptable."

"I'm still not convinced that you really are Craxton Wehl," she said primly. "They might say you are and you look like him, but you don't act like him at all. Not from the stories I've heard."

"Perhaps the operation changed me," he suggested.

"Possibly." Her eyes reflected her doubt. "Has any of your memory returned?"

"With a mindblock?"

"I thought perhaps seeing those people from your past might have awakened something."

"I catch glimpses, not what you'd call coherent ones." He grimaced at the memory of the nightmares. "Yet, when I really concentrate, the images at times become quite clear."

"If you were Craxton Wehl, you would have lived in the official residence for over thirty years. Certainly you would have some recollection of that."

He smiled at the test she was erecting for him, yet realized she was right: he had to know. He closed his eyes wearily, and forced himself to relax. Reluctantly he pushed her from his mind. For a while he was aware of the faint sounds of life from beyond the apartment; but they gradually faded from his senses. Once again he had the impression of floating in a vast, black sea.

Mr. Krant's face drifted through his mind, followed by the scent of hot chocolate. Aircars buzzed like angry wasps around the tower at the air terminal. The official residence—the Power House, they called it—sprawled in a manicured setting of lawn and stately trees. He wondered dimly how he'd known that name. He had a fleeting vision of a book-lined room, a three-view in one corner, steps that led to . . .

He groaned aloud.

"What's wrong?" she asked anxiously.

He shook his head, fighting to grasp recollections that danced like gnats around a night lamp. The stairs led to . . . a bedroom! He saw the big bed, resplendent carpeting, and drapes. A Guizaco painting adorned one wall. The painting vanished; the big bed disappeared; the carpeting and drapes faded into nothingness—he was gazing into nothing: nothing at all.

He lifted his head with a jerk and his eyes snapped open.

"What was it?" she asked worriedly.

"A library, a bedroom . . ."

"In the official residence?" she interrupted.

"I believe so."

"You've been there!" Her eyes held a touch of awe.

"So have thousands of others," he reminded.

"You should see Madelyn Wehl."

"My daughter?"

"Madelyn Wehl," she repeated. "She'd certainly know her own father."

"You still have doubts."

"Yes," she said gravely.

"And if it turns out that I am her father?"

"Then you are." Her smile was strained. "But I hope you aren't."

Later, lying in the darkness of the room, he tried to reconstruct the events as they had occurred, and to assess their meanings. Felix Quigg had been certain he was Craxton Wehl, just as he had been certain of the teleportation. And he was a teleport; he had proved that. Aside from that, he looked like Craxton Wehl.

90

But was he Craxton Wehl? The scar-faced man had been as certain as Quigg. Despite the mounting evidence, he couldn't claim the same certainty. Because of Mura's reaction? Possibly, but it went deeper. A man should react positively to his own name; it should spark his ego—set him apart as an individual different from all the rest of mankind. But he didn't react that way. He felt about the name much as he'd felt about the name Gerald Sundberg. It was a name, a tag, an identifier, but nothing more.

Why had Sundberg mindblocked him? The mindblock was the crux of the whole thing, he reflected. Was he really Craxton Wehl, former premier, or was he a pawn in some gigantic hoax? What secret had Quigg been trying to tear from behind the block?

Sundberg would know. So, perhaps, would the nurse and the attendant. One other man would know: Bernard Rayburn. For whatever reason his mind had been blocked, the order certainly had come from him. Bernard Rayburn was his sworn enemy! He clenched his fists. But Mura was right, he reflected. He had to see Madelyn Wehl. She would know; she would tell him the truth.

He found solace in the thought.

"And to the left," the tour guide droned, "we see the Wehl House."

Conscious of the stir of interest that rose from his fellow sightseers, Craxton Wehl peered through the windows of the airbus. Terraced and gabled and spired, appearing like a magic doll house set on the broad greensward, the former premier's house (his?) wheeled toward him. A swimming pool sparkled in the morning sun.

"Will we pass directly over it?" a female voice asked breathlessly.

"Private airspace," the guide answered importantly. "We'll skirt the southern border."

His ears closed to the hubbub. Wehl concentrated on the small landing pad set off to one side of the house. Rimmed by green lawn, its concrete expanse appeared an ideal target. *Teleport!* He let the word flame in his mind. He had to teleport, teleport. Vision of the rectangular landing pad danced crazily in his head. He had to . . .

A blackness gripped him. *The fish eye!* For a dancing,

fleeting second he had the impression of viewing the universe through a gigantic distorting lens. The stars thundered down. A monstrous bulk, gray and shadowy, plunged giddily into his visual field, blotting out the sky.

"*Aaaugh!*"

The woman sitting next to Wehl glanced at him in alarm. Suddenly she screamed; his seat was empty.

Pandemonium erupted on the bus.

"*Aaaugh!*"

The terrible sound ripped from his throat again, tearing away the veil of blackness. His eyes blinked open; he found himself staring upward into an azure sky. Off to one side, the receding airbus appeared small and far away.

Aching and trembling, he pushed himself to a sitting position and looked around just as a guard erupted from the doorway of the air tower. Brandishing a blaster, the man sprinted toward him. Wehl struggled painfully to his feet.

"Stand where you are," the guard shouted. Wehl waited calmly. The guard skidded to a halt a few yards away. "How'd you get here?" he demanded. His jowly face held a perplexed look.

"Put away that weapon and lower your voice," Wehl commanded sternly. "Take me to my daughter."

"Daughter?" The guard gaped at him.

"I'm Craxton Wehl." He drew his thin body straighter.

"Mr. Wehl?" The guard stared at him. "My God, you are!" He shoved the blaster from sight.

"Now take me to my daughter."

"Yes, certainly." The guard fumbled with his wrist radio and spoke haltingly into it, then stared worriedly toward the air tower. Wehl smiled, wishing he could read the man's thoughts.

A second guard popped hurriedly into view and came toward them. Golden sunbursts on his shoulder pads marked his senior position. His face, as he approached, held a quizzical, studied expression. He said in a strained voice, "Welcome, Mr. Wehl. Miss Wehl is being apprised of your, ah, arrival."

"Thank you," he answered courteously.

"We, ah, weren't informed of your visit or we would have been outside to meet you." The guard's eyes were questioning.

"I arrived rather unexpectedly," he admitted. His tone closed the conversation.

The guard shifted uncomfortably until his wrist radio pinged. He held it to his ear, listened, then dropped his arm and said, "If you would please follow me."

"Thank you," Wehl acknowledged. He followed the other through a gardened patio past the blue pool he had seen from the air. Several sunbathers on the opposite side watched him indolently. He was led into an opulent room overfilled with *objets d'art* and invited to sit. The guard hovered nearby as he dropped into a comfortable chair.

Waiting, his eyes took in the costly statuary and the rare paintings that hung from the walls. A Reimer and a Krantz—the old twenty-third century masterpieces. How did he know that? He gazed at a Martian tapestry that depicted the domes of New Seattle rising from the stark red plain of Syrtis Major. Beyond, coppery against the black sky, rose the jagged Crojyk hills.

The scene stirred his memory. Had he seen those domes before, or was he recalling the tapestry itself? The uncertainty left him baffled. Abruptly he turned, staring toward a gilded staircase. *She was coming!* His heart began to hammer.

A moment later the guard snapped to rigid attention. A stately blonde woman came into view at the top of the stairs and started down. *How had he known she was coming?* The knowledge had come in the same way it had when he'd sensed the presence of the nurse and attendant in the sky clinic. Had his mind reached out and touched hers? He rose awkwardly.

"Father!" She hurried her step. His quick glance took in her pale blue eyes, the narrow bridge of the nose, the set of her jaw—a certain tightness around the mouth. It was an imperious face, cold and artificial beneath the strained smile, yet the lines undeniably were those of his own face.

"I've been so worried," she exclaimed. Clasping his hands, she kissed his cheek lightly before stepping back to survey him.

"It's true, you're my daughter?" he asked wonderingly.

"Of course, you poor dear."

He gazed at her, making a conscious effort to read her mind. Nothing came through. "I've been having trouble with my memory," he said finally.

"Oh, it'll pass." She dismissed the guard with a curt nod. "Dr. Sundberg assured me of that," she added.

"I hope so." He contemplated the prospect wistfully. "Now and then I catch glimpses of the past."

"What kind of glimpses?"

"Things seem familiar, like that Martian tapestry on the wall."

"It's hung there for years," she exclaimed. "You've seen it hundreds of times."

"There are other things, like Mr. Krant's candy shop."

"Candy shop?"

"A small place on Glade Avenue. It's not there now."

"Perhaps that's your imagination."

"No, I remember Mr. Krant well. He was old, white-haired, always smiling. I still remember the smell of the hot chocolate." He peered at her. "Why would I remember that?"

"The memory is a warehouse of odds and ends," she explained. "Some events, even trivial ones, seem to hang on forever."

"Memory presupposes past reality," he observed.

"It's also tricky." She smiled brightly.

"Tricky and unreliable. I'm not certain that I know what reality is. Perhaps my being here is a dream." He paused. "Did you know that I'm a teleport?"

"I couldn't believe it at first," she admitted. "I thought something dreadful had happened, that Sundberg was using that as an excuse to explain your disappearance. It's still shocking, but I accept it—I have to after the manner of your arrival. Sundberg said the power must have been potential, that in some way the surgery freed it, brought it to life."

"What else did Sundberg tell you?"

"About what?"

"Did he tell you he mindblocked me?"

"That's not true," she cried. "You were suffering delusions; that's why you consulted Sundberg. He found a small brain tumor and removed it. That's what brought on the amnesia."

"Sundberg lied," he replied quietly. "I have been mindblocked." Stilling her protest, he told her what he'd overheard while under narcohypnosis in Meador's sanitarium.

"It's still not true," she exclaimed, when he'd finished.

"Perhaps they intended you to hear. It could have been a form of shock therapy, an attempt to jolt you from your amnesia."

"Why would Quigg attempt that?"

"Quigg!" She tossed her head. "That man's dangerous. I'll have him on Pluto before he knows it."

"It's not worth it." He gazed at her. "Also, someone tried to murder me."

"Murder you?" Her face turned ashen. He told her about the scar-faced man. Her eyes narrowed, and she watched him intently.

"He suggested that perhaps Rayburn had tricked me," he ended.

"Ridiculous!"

"He hinted that perhaps the transition ceremony had never occurred, that Rayburn had pulled some sort of a coup."

"That's a lie," she cried. "I witnessed it. So did half a dozen others, including Colonel Hom, of your personal security."

"I'm only repeating what he said," he remonstrated.

"Of course." She eyed him speculatively. "He must have been one of Franckel's agents."

"I've considered that."

"Your life's in danger. It's imperative that you return to Dr. Sundberg immediately."

"Why?"

"Rayburn's dying, surely you know that. If he dies without returning the power to you, Franckel will seize it. Oh, that was Franckel's man, all right. He'd do anything to prevent you from returning."

"Return the power to a mindblocked man?" He smiled wistfully.

"But you're not. It's simple amnesia. Dr. Sundberg can cure you easily enough."

"No, there's something else." He shook his head. "Something about my memories. The fish eye—or perhaps it's a nightmare."

"Fish eye?" Her head jerked up quickly. "What's that?"

"I don't know," he admitted. "It's like looking at a universe that's distorted, pulled and twisted in a crazy fashion. You should see the stars—they burn with a harsh light, then a blob races in and wipes them out."

"That's fantasy, part of the delusion," she said. "I'm certain Sundberg can explain it."

"Do you believe I'm crazy?"

"Certainly not, you poor dear. You've been ill, that's all." She forced a smile. "But all that will pass. Why don't we go to the House of Hope right now? I'll take you."

"Not yet." He shook his head decisively.

"You can't delay!" she cried.

"Because of Rayburn's condition?"

"Partially."

"What else?"

"Because of your health," she whispered.

"What about my health?"

"I haven't wanted to alarm you."

"Tell me," he commanded.

"You might die unless you return. That's why I've been so worried."

"Die of what?"

"You were taking a medicine vital to your recovery when you vanished. Without it, well . . ."

"Did Sundberg say that?"

"That you would die? He said it was possible. Oh, can't you see, you have to return."

He shook his head. "Not until I find out for certain who I am."

"Do you still doubt your identity?"

"I'm puzzled," he admitted.

"Don't you believe I'd know my own father? Look at me! Can't you see that I'm your daughter? Wait, I'll bring a mirror." She fled from the room before he could protest. The encounter left him confused. Her story was the same as Quigg's, and it was entirely logical. It also explained the scar-faced man's attempt to murder him.

But what of the mindblock? What of the bizarre universe he saw through the distorted lens of the fish eye? She'd denied one, had given a weak explanation for the other. It was easy enough to call them delusions. Aside from that, what had Quigg tried to dig from his mind? She hadn't answered that.

His visit had been useless, he reflected. He knew no more now than before he had come. Except that he had a daughter. He felt his puzzlement return. True, the resemblance was startling, but that was all. Her presence had evoked no memory, no feeling of kinship. In all but name and appearance she was an absolute stranger. And she was cold, calculating—he'd sensed that behind her brittle smile. Or had years of power made her that way? Perhaps, before the surgery, he'd been the same. Certainly he hadn't been held in much esteem.

"Mura." He uttered the name wistfully. Of all the people he'd encountered since his awakening, only she wasn't trying to use him. The rest were attempting to manipulate him for their own good. Even Madelyn. He was convinced of that. Madelyn viewed him as a lever to her own power. He smiled bitterly.

A stir came from the next room. An instant later Madelyn returned, followed by the guard with the sunbursts on his shoulders. Her face wore a flossy smile.

"You have to return to Sundberg's," she announced. "I've made arrangements."

"But I don't want to return." He struggled to his feet.

"Father!"

"I won't return!"

"It's for your own good."

"No!"

"You're ill."

"I'm not ill!" he shouted.

"Look, you're trembling." She gestured and the guard stepped suddenly forward. His hand came up with a hypodermic needle.

Wehl felt a sudden fright. *Mura! Mura!* He screamed the name in his mind. He had to teleport! The interior of her apartment danced crazily in his mind. A rough hand clasped his arm. "Wait, I'll go," he cried.

"Wait," Madelyn commanded. The guard dropped the arm and stepped back. Wehl shook the fog from his mind, concentrating on his room at Mura's. God, why couldn't he teleport? He had to, he had to. Concentration plus destination—but where was the trigger? He had to tele . . .

Blackness smashed at his mind.

Madelyn gasped, threw a hand to her mouth. The spot where Wehl had stood was empty. Frightened, she looked at the guard.

His eyes blinked stupidly.

Bernard Rayburn clicked off the radiophone, punched a button on his desk, and waited impatiently. His secretary appeared within seconds. "Have Colonel Hom come to my office immediately," he snapped.

"Yes, sir," she whispered worriedly. Watching her withdraw, he fought against the weakness permeating his body. Each day it became more pronounced. For the last week his hands, large and powerful, had trembled incessantly. One week to live! That was Sundberg's latest verdict. One week! Before that time he had to find Craxton Wehl, return the power. Only Wehl was jumping all over the landscape like a grasshopper. He sighed tiredly.

The secretary returned to the door. "Colonel Hom," she announced.

The olive-faced agent brushed past her. "Good morning, Mr. Premier."

"Sit down," Rayburn ordered brusquely. He gestured toward a chair. "Madelyn Wehl just called. She had a visitor."

"Craxton Wehl?"

"He teleported to her place."

Hom grimaced. "He appears to be getting quite adept at it. What happened?"

"I'll have to backtrack. Felix Quigg managed to snag Wehl and took him to a private sanitarium. The doctor told Quigg that Wehl had been mindblocked. Despite his drugged state, Wehl remembered that. When he shook off the drug, he teleported."

"I'm aware of that," Hom stated. "I assigned Leo Sobel to keep on Quigg's heels. Sobel possesses some excellent electronic equipment."

"Has he discovered anything?"

"Wehl previously had consulted a peeper, an illegal named Obie Frye. Frye tried to sell information to Quigg, who was smart enough to put the fellow on his payroll."

"What kind of information?" Rayburn tried to quell his alarm.

"On Wehl's whereabouts."

"Anything else?"

"Not that I know. Frye couldn't penetrate Wehl's mind."

"Couldn't break through the amnesia, eh?" Rayburn felt relieved.

"Or the mindblock—if one exists."

"It doesn't," he snapped. "His amnesia could very well be mistaken for a mindblock."

"By a medical doctor? That's difficult to believe." Hom drummed his fingers against the arm of the chair. "Quigg apparently was trying to probe Wehl's mind."

"You're saying?" Rayburn eyed the agent carefully.

"What's Quigg after?"

"I couldn't say, but that's your bailiwick," Rayburn returned. He smiled mirthlessly. "Wehl also told Madelyn that someone tried to blast him while he was in the sanitarium."

"An assassination attempt?" Hom stiffened. "Sobel missed that one."

"A scar-faced man," Rayburn pursued. His finger indicated a slashed cheek.

Hom's manner grew quiet. "That would be Sobel," he said finally.

"You don't appear surprised."

"Few things hold surprise," he admitted. "I take it that Franckel has reached him."

"Sobel scents the shift of power," Rayburn commented acidly. "He's trying to feather his future."

"What exactly happened?"

"At the sanitarium?" Rayburn frowned. "Before the assassination attempt, Sobel indicated he believed there might be something underhanded about the succession ceremony. He appeared to doubt that Wehl surrendered the Big Power Seat voluntarily."

"What would give him that idea?"

"I can't imagine." Rayburn's tone dismissed the point. "What are you going to do about Sobel?

"Nothing."

"Nothing?"

"Perhaps I can gain more that way. If Sobel's guilty, he'll hang himself; double agents usually do." Hom gazed at the premier. "What happened at Miss Wehl's?"

"She tried to convince Wehl to return. He refused."

"Did he give a reason?"

"He doubts that he's Craxton Wehl."

"Even after seeing his own daughter?"

Rayburn nodded. "When he balked, Madelyn tried to convince him with a narco needle. That was a mistake, of course. He teleported." His tone became crisp. "I haven't much time, Hom."

"I regret my failure to date." Hom inclined his head. "It isn't simple to snare a teleport, nor to hold one once you get him."

"You're saying?"

"Wehl must be convinced that he has to return."

Rayburn asked sourly, "How can you convince him if you can't catch him?"

"The leads are multiplying," the agent answered obliquely. "We know his area of operations. But in the end, I believe, he'll have to convince himself."

"Explain that."

"He's a man seeking his own identity and he won't be satisfied until he's certain of it. Everything indicates that. Look how he's hopped around, how he's tried to obtain a name. For a while he claimed to be Gerald Sundberg."

"Why that name?" asked Rayburn.

"Perhaps from some shadowy recollection." Hom made a steeple with his hands. "Any name is better than no name. Can you imagine the utter desperation of a man who has no name? With no name he has no ego, nothing on which to build. He's a cipher in the stream of life. But once he's convinced that he's Craxton Wehl, I believe he'll return of his own accord."

"If his daughter can't convince him, who can?"

Hom gazed at him. "Perhaps you can."

"I?" Rayburn considered it. "You have to find him first."

"Yes, of course."

"How do you propose to do that?"

"Through Quigg. He snatched him once. I have scant doubt but that he knows where Wehl might be found."

"Will Quigg talk?"

"When I mention Pluto, yes, he'll talk." Hom nodded.

"And then?"

"I'll contact Wehl, urge him to see you."

"Do you believe he would?"

"If it meant erasing the doubts concerning his identity, yes."

"I hope it works." Rayburn sighed and leaned back. "But hurry," he pleaded.

"I'll get the truth," Hom promised.

"Just get Wehl back."

The agent started to reply, then murmured good-bye and left. Riding the elevator to his office, he wondered again on what basis Quigg's doctor had pronounced Wehl mindblocked, and why Wehl still doubted his own identity. Of one thing he was certain: there was far more to the story than Rayburn had admitted.

TEN

Wehl awoke, blinking in a shaft of afternoon light that filtered in through the curtains. Mura's apartment! The silence told him he was alone. As he pushed himself to a sitting position, the memories rushed back.

Craxton Wehl! Incredible as it seemed, he was Craxton Wehl, former premier of the Solar Empire. Bernard Rayburn was dying, wanted to return him to power! That was more incredible yet. Or had Rayburn tricked him of the power, now wanted to kill him? And Madelyn! He winced at the memory of their meeting. She had tried to trick him, too. His own daughter!

He rose unsteadily and went to the couch. Madelyn had warned that he might die unless he returned to the sky clinic. Or was that more trickery? He buried his face in his hands. For a short while he'd derived satisfaction from simply being Gerald Sundberg, then the name had been ripped ruthlessly from him; he had become Craxton Wehl. Now he was caught in a conspiracy that lay beyond his understanding.

Who knew the real truth? Not Felix Quigg, not the scar-faced man; they'd tried to pump him. Gerald Sundberg knew, he thought coldly. So did Bernard Rayburn, and perhaps Madelyn. They were using him as a pawn.

He went to the window, drew aside the curtain, and gazed at the tower that marked the space terminal, then swept his vision along the shops and apartments lining

Glade Avenue. The sight stirred shadowy memories from long, long ago.

His eyes closed, he concentrated in an attempt to make the memories burn more brightly. He had to solidify them, link them together to give continuity to his past. He sensed that in some way the fish eye and Mr. Krant's candy shop were linked, but how? Why had he first tele-ported to Mura's? The question seemed unanswerable. He sensed the memories fading, and groaned.

Gerald Sundberg! He clenched his fists. He had to see Sundberg! *But wasn't that what everyone wanted, for him to see Sundberg?* It was, of course, but if Sundberg knew the answer? He had no alternative; he had to see Sundberg! He drew the stun gun from his pocket and eyed it curiously. If he saw Sundberg, it would be on his own terms. And Sundberg would talk; he'd make him!

He glanced at the clock. Mura would be home almost any minute. He decided against waiting for her and re-turned to the couch. His eyes closed, he shut his ears to the sounds from the street. For a few seconds he was content to drift in the solitude of his mind, then finally resurrected a vision of the small cubicle he had inhabited in the sky clinic.

Teleport, teleport, teleport. The word ran like a whisper through his mind as he conjured up a vision of the barren room with its sterile walls and ceiling—the cot jammed into one corner. *Teleport, teleport* ... He was Craxton Wehl, former premier; Craxton Wehl, teleport. *Teleport, teleport* ...

A scream penetrated his consciouness. Mura! Dimly he knew it was she. As he struggled to break his self-induced trance, he sensed the world reel and dance madly around him; the blackness flooded in.

He awoke, almost instantly it seemed, with no recollec-tion of the passage of time. The floor was cold and hard. The sterile walls rising closely around him and the white cot fitted neatly into a corner told him he'd returned to his cubicle in the sky clinic.

His heart thudded, and he trembled violently. The weakness which gripped him made him wonder at the stresses involved in propelling himself from the Earth's surface to a destination high in orbit. Did he travel as a totality, shoot like a meteor through space? Or did his

102

atoms disassociate, stream with the swiftness of light, recombine once he'd reached his mind-chosen goal? The questions awed him.

He recalled Mura's startled cry and grimaced. She must have entered the apartment just in time to see him vanish. That could be quite a shock. He pushed the thought aside and lurched to his feet, fighting to retain his balance. Although the anti-gravs in space acted to create an artificial gravity, he had the sensation of floating. He cocked his head to listen. Except for the low hum of an air fan, the clinic was absolutely silent. Suppose Sundberg was gone again? The possibility dismayed him.

"Aaahhh!" The high, piercing scream, bouncing off the metal walls, shattered the stillness. He recoiled, his first thought that he had been discovered wiped away by the realization that the cry had come from behind one of the closed doors across the corridor. The surgery, he thought.

"Aaahhh!" The shriek came again, followed by a racking sob. Frightened, he pulled the stun gun from his pocket.

"Teleport, teleport," he told himself, "get away while you can." Despite his anxiety, he stood fast, determined not to leave without the answers to his questions. He stared nervously at the door to the surgery.

"Stop, you're killing me!" a voice screamed. He stiffened. Sundberg . . . torturing someone? His hands began to shake.

"Talk, damn you!" The second voice, taut and flat, brought up his head with a jerk. He knew that voice! Somewhere, at some time, he'd heard it. When? Where? He fought vainly to place it.

"Wehl passed the power, he passed the power," the first voice screamed. *"I told you that! He passed the power and a dozen people saw him do it!"*

"To Bernard Rayburn?" the flat voice asked insistently. Wehl twitched violently as if a trigger had been pulled in his mind. The scar-faced man! He knew that voice now— could all but see the curving white slash that pulled the thin-lipped mouth awry, the glittering dark eyes that had stared at him in Meador's clinic.

"Yes, yes, he passed it to Rayburn."

"Then why was Wehl mindblocked? Talk, Kelsey, it's

103

your last chance!" The attendant! Wehl suppressed his shock.

"*I don't know, I don't know,*" Kelsey moaned.

"*You know he was mindblocked!*"

"*No! No! Lord, the pain, I can't stand it.*"

"*You were here when the surgery was performed. So was the nurse.*"

"*Then ask her,*" Kelsey wailed.

"*Don't try to be cute, Kelsey. That stunner knocked her cold.*"

"*I don't . . . Oh, God, don't! I can't stand any more!*"

"*Talk!*"

"*I don't know, I don't . . . Aaahhhhhh!*"

"*Is Rayburn really dying?*"

"*Yes, yes, Europa fever, I told you. That's where Sundberg is now . . . treating him.*"

"*Nice story,*" the scar-faced man rasped nastily. "*Let's try the scapel again.*"

"*It's the truth . . . Aaahhhhh!*"

"*The real truth, Kelsey. Quick!*"

"*Don't, don't, I can't stand it! God, the pain!*" The anguished sob from the surgery tore at Wehl's mind. Battered by warring emotions, he stared indecisively at the door. The scar-faced man was trying to elicit the very information he'd come to get, yet he couldn't stand by and do nothing—the tortured screams were too much.

He gripped the stun gun and stole across the corridor. Grasping the doorknob gently, he tried to turn it. Locked! Another scream came from inside, followed by the scar-faced man's demanding voice. Wehl writhed in an agony of indecision.

"*Teleport! Teleport!* The word thundered in his brain. He closed his eyes and concentrated on the interior of the surgery as he recalled it. The operating table under the bank of bright lights, the small sink and cabinets built along the walls—the image grew in his mind. If Kelsey were on the table, the chances were that the scar-faced man's back would be to him—if he reappeared just inside the door. If the scar-faced man saw him first! He shuddered. But he had to chance it!

"*Teleport, teleport!*" He screamed the word in his mind. *Kelsey was on the table!* The momentary vision of the

104

man, the table, and the white lights filled his consciousness. Almost as abruptly it began to fade, was gone.

"Teleport, teleport!" The word became a frantic clamor in his brain. He had the giddy sensation of crumpling, disintegrating—the world around him danced and spun; blackness, like a tidal wave, rushed in to engulf him.

Almost instantly his eyes opened; almost instantly he was aware of lying half-propped against a wall. A few yards away a man's broad back, turned toward him, was bent over a figure on the operating table.

He shook his head to clear his eyes. The figure on the table was Kelsey, all right. His hands and feet were covered with blood. Another scream came. Loud and piercing, it echoed with pain and despair. Wehl fumbled with the stun gun and struggled to his feet.

"Stop!" As the strangled command burst from his lips, he saw the scar-faced man whirl, a hand darting toward a pocket. "Stop or I'll shoot," Wehl cried.

The scar-faced man's hand stopped in midair. "Craxton Wehl!" He uttered the name with disbelief.

"Wehl!" Kelsey called, his voice choked. He struggled against the straps that held him to the table. "Shoot him before he kills us both."

"Shut up!" the scar-faced man snarled. His glittering eyes fixed Wehl. "I'm here to help you."

"Help me?" Wehl was aghast.

"Don't believe him," screamed Kelsey. "He's a liar!"

The scar-faced man disregarded him. "You're the victim of a plot, Wehl. This fellow is in on it, or at least knows of it."

Wehl regarded the other coldly. "What's your interest?"

"You don't remember me?" The scar-faced man gave a tight-lipped smile. "I'm Leon Sobel, of the premier's personal security. Colonel Hom assigned me to the case."

"Who's Colonel Hom?"

"Chief of the premier's security."

"He witnessed the succession ceremony," shouted Kelsey.

"He believes the ceremony was rigged," Sobel stated. "That's why I'm here, to get at the truth of things."

"A lie, a lie," the attendant shrieked.

"It is a lie," said Wehl. "You tried to kill me."

"That was an act," Sobel responded. "I was trying to jolt you out of your amnesia."

Wehl stared incredulously at him. "Do you expect me to believe that?"

"It's the truth, Wehl. You were mindblocked, you know that. Do you know why?"

Wehl eyed him steadily. "You tell me."

"Rayburn tricked you; I discovered that. The succession ceremony wasn't legal."

"The proof?" he snapped.

"Rayburn wasn't Earth-born. That makes him ineligible. He engineered the story that his birth certificate was stolen to hide the fact that he was born in Europa. The colony government went along with it, provided a supposed copy of the original document to get their man into power."

"Fantastic," he exclaimed.

"That's what Quigg was trying to verify when he had the doc milk your brain."

"Don't listen to him," Kelsey shouted wildly. "It's all a pack of lies!"

"You'll scream your way to Pluto," Sobel snarled. His gaze swung back to Wehl. "You discovered Rayburn's duplicity too late. That's why Sundberg had you mindblocked—to keep you from remembering."

"If that's true, why didn't he have me killed?"

"That's what he's trying to do now, Wehl." Sobel's words were calm and straightforward. "At first he was afraid to have you murdered, afraid of possible political repercussions. He had to have time to solidify his power base. Now he's afraid that his enemies might get hold of you, have the block removed. You have a lot of friends who want to see justice done, Wehl. I know, they're helping push this investigation."

"Franckel?"

Sobel's gaze flickered. "Franckel's interested in honest government," he said finally.

"Then Rayburn's not dying?"

"Dying?" Sobel laughed harshly. "No, he's not dying. That's the story to get you to return here."

"So they can kill me?"

Sobel jerked his head affirmatively. "Sundberg is slated to finish the job."

"Don't listen to him," cried Kelsey. "It's not true, none of it. Rayburn has Europa fever; I know that."

"Europa fever!" Sobel snickered.

"My own daughter told me that," said Wehl.

"Oh!" Sobel looked suddenly wary.

"She told me Rayburn wanted to return the power to prevent Franckel from seizing it."

"Your daughter's ambitious," Sobel answered woodenly.

"Meaning?"

"She's thrown in her lot with Rayburn."

"Against her own father?" he demanded.

"I don't want to enter into your family affairs but, yes, she has, although it's quite possible she doesn't realize that Rayburn intends to kill you." Sobel's voice held a reasonable edge. "If you proved Rayburn's duplicity and regained the power, how long would you hold it? A few years at most. But Rayburn's young, could retain his hold for another thirty or forty years. Your daughter is acutely aware of that, Wehl. Power is the coin of bribery; you certainly realize that."

"Does Colonel Hom know all this?"

Sobel hesitated only a second. "Not yet."

"Why not?"

"I haven't completed my report."

"A lie," shouted Kelsey. "Hom was here when the ceremony was held. Don't listen to him."

Wehl kept his eyes on Sobel's face. "Why the delay?"

"In making the report?" Sobel's smile was strained. "I'm trying to tie up the loose ends. If I don't, the report will never see the light of day, but it could very well take me to Pluto."

"Hom witnessed the succession ceremony," he reminded.

"Oh, I'm not denying that."

"What are you trying to say?"

"You didn't go there for the ceremony," Sobel explained. "You went there for treatment. Sundberg put you under hypnosis, implanted the idea that you wanted to pass the power—programmed the whole thing in your mind. Then Rayburn showed up with Hom and the others as witnesses and—presto!—you were out and he was in."

"Why would Rayburn do that if I'd already selected him as my successor?"

107

"He couldn't wait, Wehl."

"Why not?"

"You brought him here as a possible successor, even probable, I might say. His role was that of an understudy. You didn't intend to pass the power immediately; the plan was long-range. But you began to perceive gaps in his character, to gather doubts."

"How would you know that?" Wehl interrupted.

"The grapevine." Sobel shrugged. "Those things get around. That's why Rayburn acted so abruptly."

"Lies," shouted Kelsey.

Sobel swung toward him. "This guy was in on it, Wehl. You came here to get information, didn't you? Well, so did I."

"Not by torture."

"He's expendable."

"No one's expendable, Sobel. I'm going to hold you both here until Sundberg returns, persuade him—by force, if necessary—to do a bit of psycho-probing."

"Would he psycho-probe his own man?"

"I was referring to you."

"What?" Sobel's eyes narrowed.

"I might get at the real truth that way," said Wehl. "At least it would be a starter."

"I'll give him the needle myself," yelled Kelsey.

"That's not necessary." The tautness slipped like a cape from Sobel's body. "I'm perfectly agreeable to examination under the lie detector."

"You are?" Wehl was startled.

"I want you to be convinced." Sobel glanced toward the door. "Quiet, someone's coming."

As Wehl cocked his head to listen, the agent's hand darted to a pocket and came out with a blaster. Wehl was quicker. Jerking his finger against the trigger, he felt the recoil as a force field leaped out to catch Sobel squarely in the chest. The agent reeled backward, his face glazed. Half-turning, he slowly bent forward before toppling to the floor.

"Got him," the attendant exulted.

"Stunned," Wehl said in a strangled voice. His hands shook.

"Put it to his head," yelled Kelsey. "Scramble his brains."

"Why?" He glanced back at the attendant's bloody figure.

"Look what he did to me! My God, the pain! He pushed those scapels under my fingernails and toenails—inched them in bit by bit. Kill him while you have the chance."

Wehl shook his head. "You're too anxious."

"Anxious? He's a killer, a sadist. Sure I want him dead." Kelsey shuddered. "I don't want him to have another chance at me."

Wehl regarded the attendant appraisingly. "Is Rayburn dying?"

"I told you that. Unstrap me, Wehl. I need a painkiller."

"Europa fever?"

"Sure, what else?"

"Have you seen him since its onset?"

"He came here for examination. He was half-dead, Wehl."

"What were the symptoms?"

"Of Europa fever?" Kelsey looked startled. "You're trying to trick me," he accused.

"I'm asking you."

"I can't talk, Wehl. I'm in agony."

"You're hiding something!"

"I'm not, I tell you, I'm not. What gives you that idea?"

"I sense it."

"Sense it?"

"I'm a teleport," said Wehl. "Did you know that?"

"Yes, sure, that's how you broke out of this trap. I hear you've been bouncing all over the place."

"Did you know that I'm a telepath?"

"You . . . a telepath?" Kelsey recoiled, frightened.

"Of course." The lie came easily. "What's so strange about that, Kelsey? Teleportation takes a much greater power."

"Telepath," Kelsey mumbled.

"Now answer my questions," he ordered sternly.

"But if you're a telepath . . . ?" Disbelief crept into the attendant's eyes.

"I'm trying to tie the loose ends together," Wehl supplied smoothly. "There are things that aren't in your mind

109

unless I ask you. The questions bring them to your conscious attention. Now, is Rayburn dying?"

"Yes, I said so."

"Europa fever?"

"I can't tell you," Kelsey gasped.

"Why not?"

"I have a family, Wehl."

"So?"

"If I squawk, they'll butcher me."

"They?"

"I won't talk, won't think. You're wasting your time."

"I'll be back in the Big Power Seat before the week is out, Kelsey."

"Yeah, maybe."

"Maybe?"

"You might be dead, Wehl."

"Oh?" Wehl pursed his lips, remembering what Madelyn had said. "Unless I come back for treatment, is that it?"

"That's right." Kelsey avoided his eyes.

"You're lying, Kelsey." The look of discomfiture on the attendant's face told him that his shot in the dark had struck the target. Was he dying? He forced his attention back to the figure on the table and said, "How would you like to wind up on Pluto?"

"That threat doesn't scare me."

"You believe I won't put you there?"

"I'm not talking."

"No?" asked Wehl softly. He studied the other curiously. If Kelsey weren't afraid, it must be through the certainty that he would never possess the power to send him to Pluto. He put the thought into words.

"I'm through talking," Kelsey stated flatly.

"I don't have to be premier to have the power to send you to Pluto," Wehl returned.

"No?"

"I can make that as part of the deal for returning."

"No!" Kelsey screamed. He turned his face to the wall.

"I'll demand that they send your whole family."

"My God!" Kelsey's head jerked back, his eyes filled with horror. "You can't do a thing like that, Wehl. You can't!"

"Can't?" Wehl pressed his advantage. "Do you know what it's like out there? The sun lies so far away that it's

110

less than a firefly in the sky—so remote that its light gives no day. The cold is incredible. Have you heard of the Pastures of Pluto? Frozen ammonia and methane, Kelsey. That's where the exile domes are—peeping out from seas of frozen gas. Small wonder the inhabitants all go mad. They're less than animals out there, Kelsey. Did you know . . . ?"

"Stop!" Kelsey shrieked.

"You'll talk?"

"I don't know what's killing Rayburn. That's the truth. I only know what Sundberg says—the man's dying. He claims it's Europa fever. But how would I know, Wehl? I never heard of a case on Earth before. Do you think I'd take a chance on lying to a peeper, or to Hom? That guy would fry me in a second."

"Colonel Jing Lee Hom?" Wehl suppressed his surprise.

"Give me a pain-killer," Kelsey groaned. He gestured with his head. "That green bottle on the shelf. Plunk two in my mouth. Hurry, I can't stand much more of this."

Wehl shook two tablets into his hand. "Water?"

"Just the pills."

"What did Hom want?"

"He was curious about why Rayburn had been brought here, why he's dying."

"Chief of the premier's security and he didn't know? What did you tell him?"

"That he'd have to talk to Sundberg. I wasn't about to squawk."

"Close-mouthed, aren't you?"

"I've got a family, Wehl. God, give me those pills. This pain is getting worse by the minute."

Wehl balanced them in his hand. "I'm not satisfied with your story, Kelsey. No pills till you talk."

"You're as bad as Sobel," the attendant exclaimed bitterly.

"I'm getting that way."

"Give me the pills and I'll talk."

"Is that a promise?"

"Would a man in my shape lie?"

"Peeping you, I'd say yes."

"My mind's a liar," Kelsey shrieked. "The agony makes me think all sorts of crazy things. I don't know the truth."

111

"Who does?" Wehl demanded.

"Sundberg!"

"Who else?"

"Bernard Rayburn!"

"Who else?"

"How would I know?"

"Does Madelyn Wehl know?"

"Your daughter?"

"I'm not so certain that she is," Wehl confessed.

"Ha!"

"What does that mean?"

"The pills," Kelsey croaked.

"You'll keep talking?"

"As much as I know."

"I'm taking you on trust." Wehl displayed the pills in his palm.

"Drip them in my mouth," the attendant gasped. Wehl extended his palm and tilted it, watched the pills fall between Kelsey's lips. Kelsey gulped, swallowed convulsively. *"Aahhh!"* A sigh of relief came from his lips.

"Do they help?"

"Yeah, sure, wait'll they take effect." Kelsey closed his eyes.

Wehl had a horrible premonition. "What kind of pills were those?" he shouted.

"A real knockout."

"Knockout?" he demanded.

"Sleeping pills. They've got the kick of a mule."

"Talk, damn you." He grasped the attendant's shoulder and shook it roughly. "Talk or I'll send your family to Pluto by personal express; I promise you that, Kelsey."

"It . . . fogs the mind."

"You're lying, you're trying to trick me!"

"Please, I can't stay awake." Kelsey's voice took on a dreamy quality as the tautness fled from his face.

"Talk," yelled Wehl frantically.

"You . . . don't know anything," Kelsey murmured. "You're guessing . . . guessing." His eyes fluttered several times and closed.

"What don't I know?"

"I'm . . . getting sleepy."

"I'd like to reach down your throat and yank those damned pills back," he exclaimed savagely. He fought to

112

control his panic. What didn't he know? Whatever it was, Kelsey knew; he knew and it was something too frightful to reveal to Sobel, even under torture. "Talk," he screamed again.

Kelsey struggled to open his eyes. "You're dead, Wehl."

"If I don't give myself up to Sundberg?"

"Dead . . . ha!" The exclamation on his lips, Kelsey turned his face toward the wall. Wehl shook him vigorously, was rewarded by a nasal snore. He jerked Kelsey's head around and opened one lid; the eye was glazed and blank. Baffled, he swung toward Sobel. The agent's breath came in a harsh wheeze that told Wehl the man would be out for hours.

What now? He gazed around despairingly. He was dead; suddenly he knew it. He felt it in every muscle and bone and nerve in his body. He knew it and Kelsey had known it. Well, before he died he was going to find out who he was, why his mind had been blocked.

He brushed his face wearily. He hadn't much time, not much time. He had to see Mura again. The desire mounted. Of all the teeming billions in this world, only she could be trusted. *"Mura, Mura, Mura."* He closed his eyes and concentrated.

An instant later he was in her apartment.

ELEVEN

"I can't believe you're Craxton Wehl," Mura stated. "I've never believed it. Would your own daughter try to trick you?"

"Perhaps she thought it was for my own good," he reflected.

"You don't believe that."

"No, not really."

"Did you try . . . ?" She paused, as if wondering how to proceed.

113

"To read her mind?" He nodded. "Nothing came through."

"Nothing at all?"

"Not even a glimmer." He hesitated. "But I did sense her before she entered the room; I knew she was coming, and from which direction. It was like knowing the whereabouts of Kelsey and the nurse in the sky clinic.

"Perhaps the talent is just developing."

"But why so slowly?" He gestured helplessly. "The teleportation came quickly enough."

"It could be a matter of finding the right key—making the proper neural connections."

"Perhaps." He mulled the point. "But I know Madelyn's my own flesh and blood. You have but to look at her to see the heritage in her face. She's my daughter, all right, but I hate to admit it."

"I still can't believe it," she cried.

"It isn't pleasant."

"It's not that," she denied. "It's something I sense. There's something terribly wrong. The thought of your being Craxton Wehl is like a bad dream."

He smiled faintly. "Perhaps the mindblock was to cut out my meanness."

"Oh, I didn't mean that!" she exclaimed. "You're not mean or petty, nothing like that. If you were, the story might make sense. As it is . . ." She lapsed into an uneasy silence.

"Sundberg knows the answer," he mused. "Kelsey admitted that."

"Then you have to see him!"

"That's what they want; they're waiting for that to happen." He shrugged. "I've tried twice."

"Someone has to know the truth."

"Rayburn does."

"Bernard Rayburn!" She lifted her face, frightened.

"I could confront him, see his reaction."

"That would be dangerous!"

"Not if I caught him alone."

"Would that be possible?"

"In his own quarters, yes."

She eyed him worriedly. "Wouldn't you have to be able to remember?"

"His private suite? I believe I can," he asserted. "I've

thought a lot about it. I have the same sort of fleeting memories that I do when I think of the tower at the space terminal, or this room, or Mr. Krant's candy shop. I have the impression of a large room, deep gold rugs, a large bed—windows that look out on an expanse of green lawn. It holds a certain familiarity, yet it doesn't."

"What do you mean by that?"

"Memory of Mr. Krant's candy shop, other things along Glade Avenue, bring a certain nostalgia. His library and bedroom are there in my mind, but there's no nostalgia. I've been there, but I don't feel that I've ever lived there."

She asked anxiously, "What are we going to do?"

"I'm going to find out who I am."

"Then you don't really believe you are Craxton Wehl," she charged.

"Yes, I believe it." He inclined his head. "Madelyn convinced me of that, even though I wanted to deny it at the time. She was cold, false; her face held a touch of arrogance and disdain, but the lines were the lines of this face." He touched his cheek.

"What don't you believe?" she insisted.

"I'm mixed up in some kind of a giant conspiracy, Mura." He closed his eyes, rubbed his temples with his fingertips. "That I'm the victim is clear enough. Perhaps I was robbed of the Big Power Seat, I don't know. Why did Sundberg mindblock me? Again I don't know, but it could only be to still my memories. What is it I'm not allowed to remember?"

"Keep thinking," she urged.

"Why did Quigg try to probe me? To discover the secret and sell it? Why did Sobel try to kill me? To prevent my return to the Big Power Seat—clear the way for Franckel? If that surmise is correct, as it appears to be, then it must be true that Rayburn wants me to return to office. But that doesn't tie in with the mindblock. Why did Kelsey tell me I was as good as dead?"

"I don't know," she whispered.

"Madelyn told me the same thing."

"Perhaps they were trying to frighten you into returning."

"Yes, but why? That's what puzzles me. Why do they want me back?"

When she left for work, he went outside and viewed the

115

street. Memories danced like phantoms in his mind. He wondered where reality ceased and unreality began. Could this be part of the dementia that had sent him to Sundberg in the first place? He wasn't crazy! He whispered the denial fiercely. He might be old, weak, trembling, in the sundown of life, but he possessed all his faculties; all but his memory. But that, too, would return! He promised himself that.

He trudged slowly along Glade Avenue until he reached the public library. As he'd expected, there were hundreds of books and tapes on Craxton Wehl. He sampled the volumes randomly. Pictures of himself stared out at him from various periods in his life. From childhood to old age—his progress was documented in the dry pages. He had been born in Rochester, a suburb of the New York megalopolis in ...

My God, he was seventy-six years old! He brushed his cheeks in awe. Small wonder he trembled and ached and felt so weak. He was a man at the very end of life, an old man who didn't even know who or what he was. He forced his attention to the print.

His school record, if not brilliant, was quite impressive. Oratory had been his forte. Rising rapidly in politics, he had become New York's youngest mayor; in five more years, the youngest governor in the Americas before succeeding to the Big Power Seat.

He tried to picture New York, but without success. His impression was of a vast sprawl that extended from Old Boston to Virginia. He flipped through the pages. He had married an Ellen Cardon shortly before succeeding to the Big Power Seat. He probed his memory; the name meant nothing. A daughter Madelyn had been born of the issue. Nothing, nothing, nothing—his mind was blank. He scanned other books, found the facts all alien; nothing stirred his recall.

As an afterthought he scanned the index on Bernard Rayburn, then flipped through several volumes before he found himself gazing at the lean face of a blond young giant. The caption it read: ELECTED LEADER OF COLONY COUNCIL.

He perused the account unhurriedly. Just as he had been the youngest governor of the Americas, Bernard Rayburn had been the youngest person ever elected to

116

lead the government of that distant Jovian moon. His campaign slogan described his political philosophy: EQUAL POWER FOR AN EQUAL WORLD.

Equal world? He smiled. The entire population of that bleak moon barely reached—he glanced at a population figure—twenty thousand. He felt a tingle of admiration for them. Huddled in their submethane villages with only an occasional dome through which to view the starry sky, they had to bore downward to tap that small world's core for heat and metals. But their dream of greatness was only that—a dream.

Still, Rayburn's record was quite impressive. He could see why the man might have been chosen for the Big Power Seat. Certainly his selection would do much to tie the OutSat worlds to the Mother Empire.

He scanned Rayburn's personal record interestedly. In his few years Rayburn had excelled in many fields other than politics. He had gained local fame as a poet and philosopher, and for his explorations of the methane grottoes that stabbed deeply and tortuously into that moon's frozen crust. Another picture showed him with his dog, Jupe, at the dedication of a new dome; a third showed him relaxed in his den. All in all, the account gave insight into the life of a man who, heretofore, had been just a name.

He returned outside, looked at the leaden sky. Had he chosen Bernard Rayburn as his successor? His fleeting memories didn't tell him that. As he passed through Craxton Wehl Park, he halted suddenly, a sense of *presence* filling his mind. His heart commenced to hammer.

A hand touched his elbow. "Mr. Wehl?"

He turned slowly, the sweat cold on his brow. Dark Oriental eyes watched him from a slender, olive face. He realized the futility of denying the name, said tiredly, "Yes?"

"My name is Hom . . ."

"Colonel Jing Lee Hom," he interrupted. Dismay struck him.

"Ah, you remember!"

"I heard the name recently." His ire exploded. "How could I remember past your mindblock?"

"I believe you are mistaken, Mr. Wehl."

117

"There's no mistake," he cried hotly.

"I'm certain you suffer simple amnesia."

"I know better." He struggled to contain his emotions. "Sundberg's attendant admitted as much."

"He did?" Hom's scrutiny sharpened.

"His manner, his trying to dodge the issue," Wehl conceded lamely.

"Ah, but that's not the same thing." Hom regarded him professionally. "I fear he was rather distraught, Mr. Wehl. But you look tired. Shall we sit while we talk?" He gestured toward a bench. Wehl followed him numbly, wondering what lay ahead. The agent's sudden appearance gave him the impression of the world closing in—the utter impossibility of escape. Curious over what the other might have to say, he discarded the idea of teleportation.

Seated, Hom asked, "Is it true that you're telepathic?"

"Ask Kelsey," he snapped. "What do you want of me?"

"To ask you to return to Dr. Sundberg's clinic."

"Why?"

"To complete your treatment, Mr. Wehl."

"Or else, I'll die, is that it?"

"Die?" Hom's eyes were puzzled.

"If I don't return."

"What gives you that impression, Mr. Wehl?"

"My daughter Madelyn told me, and Kelsey."

"I'm not aware of such a possibility," replied Hom. "I know only that you need treatment."

"The treatment is murder," he grated.

"You have a mistaken impression."

"I have? Your man tried to murder me."

"That was regrettable."

"Did you reward Sobel or send him to Pluto for failing?"

"Neither, Mr. Wehl."

"Gave him a second chance, is that it?"

Hom shook his head. "Sobel surrendered any hope of mercy when he tried to assassinate you. He compounded his crime by trying to extract information about you from Sundberg's attendant. Fortunately for Kelsey, he recovered consciousness first, freed himself, and sent out a call for help. Had Sobel recovered first . . ." He shrugged.

Wehl suppressed a pang of guilt. "Where's Sobel now?"

"He escaped," said Hom somberly. "He knows all the

tricks. That's another reason you should return to Sundberg immediately. You're not safe as long as he's free."

"What has he to gain by killing me now?"

"Perhaps nothing, perhaps everything."

"Talk straight," snapped Wehl testily.

"Sorry, I wasn't aware that I wasn't," Hom apologized. "If your murder led to, ah, someone else gaining the power . . ."

"Sobel would be rewarded, is that it?"

"A very likely outcome—also a compelling reason why you should return to the sky clinic."

Wehl glared at the agent. "I suppose you're going to tell me that Rayburn is dying, wants to return me to power to prevent Franckel from seizing it."

"Essentially that is correct, Mr. Wehl, although I have no direct knowledge of Franckel's involvement."

"You deny that I was mindblocked?"

"Again I have no direct knowledge."

"That's an evasion, Hom."

"Yes." The agent nodded reluctantly.

Wehl's head jerked up in surprise. "You admit that?"

"Dr. Meador is convinced that it is so."

"Quigg's man? You've talked with him?"

"He was a most reluctant speaker," admitted Hom.

"If you've contemplated the possibility of a mindblock, have you contemplated its purpose?"

Hom said gravely, "I can find no purpose, Mr. Wehl. That weakens my belief that such a block exists."

"It exists," snorted Wehl. "Why should I return?"

"The premier's orders."

"Why should I obey him?"

"His order is law, Mr. Wehl. Certainly you should be the first to appreciate that."

"Why should he want me?" he cried. "I'm seventy-six years old. I'm sick, perhaps dying. At times it's an effort to stand, to walk. He knows that; Sundberg knows it. So why should he want me back? I wouldn't last long."

"Long enough to select a suitable successor, Mr. Wehl. It would circumvent the restlessness of the governors, preserve the integrity of the office. Could the premier risk making such a choice, new as he is? Never, and he realizes it."

"If I refuse?"

119

"I hope to persuade you."

"No doubt," said Wehl bitterly. He had the feeling of a deadly cat and mouse game. Yet Hom's hands were in plain sight; he appeared to offer no immediate threat. He resisted the impulse to teleport and demanded, "How did you find me?"

"Quigg, Meador, Obie Frye—your passage has not been unmarked, Mr. Wehl."

"Obie Frye?" He was startled. "How did you learn about him?"

"Quigg was thoughtful enough to employ him when he tried to sell information on your visit."

"That's a violation of the code," he snapped.

"A partial has no code, Mr. Wehl."

"Has anyone? Quigg's trying to market me all over the empire." He shook his head doggedly. "I won't return."

"It is not often that the death of a single man can shake an empire," returned Hom, "but in this instance it is so. Premier Rayburn is gravely ill. You have but a day or two to make your decision. Should you refuse to return, the decision could be fatal."

"To me or to the empire?"

"To the empire, Mr. Wehl."

"Why? The empire got along before Rayburn was ever heard of."

"Your strong hand was at the helm, and before that, a strong line of predecessors."

"That's not convincing," he answered tightly.

"I have no better argument."

He asked curiously, "Why did I choose a colonist? That doesn't make sense."

"An act of statesmanship," asserted Hom. "It was an acknowledgment of our expanding empire, a recognition that Earth couldn't subsidize the rule alone."

"Bernard Rayburn was born on Earth," he objected.

"The law still requires that." Hom nodded. "The public feeling is such that even a strong premier couldn't overturn it. But essentially Bernard Rayburn is a colonist. As such, his appointment is a step along the way."

Wehl rose. "Your story is too convincing."

"I intend to convince you," said Hom. He stood.

"I'm not certain Rayburn is the premier, or that the succession ceremony ever occurred."

"I witnessed it." A quizzical expression touched the olive face. "What do you believe?"

"I'm not certain." Wehl mulled the point. "It's possible that if the ceremony was held, it was illegal—that I was tricked of the power."

Hom shook his head in negation.

"It's also possible that a switch was made—that the man you call Rayburn is not Rayburn at all. I've considered that he might be a pawn—that the empire is being juggled by someone else. Perhaps Franckel."

"That is not the case, Mr. Wehl."

"How do you know? Did you know Rayburn before he was brought to Earth? Did you become sufficiently well acquainted with him to state absolutely that he is the man now occupying the Big Power Seat?"

"I checked quite early. His fingerprints match those of record on Europa."

"Then you had doubts," he challenged.

Hom hesitated. "Such procedures are normal. Aside from that, the premier is offering you the power—begging you to take it. Is that the act of a conspirator?"

"He's offering me death," said Wehl harshly.

"He's aware of your doubts. For that reason he wishes to convey the offer personally."

"In Sundberg's clinic, no doubt."

"At a place of your own choice."

"And if I refuse?"

"The empire will suffer."

"If you believe that, why don't you use the stun gun on me, or a narco needle? It's been done before."

"To what avail? When the shock passes, you can teleport."

"You could keep me under long enough to kill me."

"Couldn't I do that now, at this moment?"

"Too many witnesses," Wehl retorted, but he knew his words were false. Hom could kill him quite easily and no one would dare question the act—not if the agent were working on Rayburn's orders.

Hom smiled. "You perceive the fallacy of your statement," he observed. "You can always reach me through Information Central. Call when you reach a decision. But hurry, time is short."

"I've made my decision." Wehl wheeled and walked

121

away, half expecting a blaster bolt between the shoulders. The fear made him hurry. At the far end of the walk, he looked back. Hom raised a hand in gesture, then turned and departed in the opposite direction.

Wehl watched him perplexedly. Hom seemed honest enough. He'd been quick to acknowledge Sobel's dereliction. He also held questions concerning the mindblock, and Bernard Rayburn's identity. His interrogation of Meador and his check of the premier's fingerprints proved that, even though the agent had characterized the latter as a normal procedure.

Yet the man was an agent—the premier's personal agent, he corrected. Was Hom loyal to the man or to the office? Suppose that Bernard Rayburn proved an impostor. That was foolish, of course, but suppose that he did? What would Hom do then?

The thought intrigued him. If he had been tricked out of office, that was one thing; Rayburn still would be premier. The *fait accompli* was all that mattered. But suppose the succession ceremony had never occurred. In that event Craxton Wehl—himself?—still was premier. But the ceremony had occurred; Hom had witnessed it. If Hom could be believed.

He debated the point. Hom believed him possibly telepathic—he had been quick to question that. Wehl chuckled at his deception. Not that the agent was gullible; telepathy seemed a small talent when compared with teleportation. Still, not knowing, Hom scarcely would have risked lying. Wehl reached a decision: Hom had been truthful. He'd take that as a starter.

Where did that leave him? He ruefully pursed his lips. Quigg was trying to sell him, Sobel was trying to murder him, Bernard Rayburn was trying to give him the Solar Empire. Quigg's motives were easily understood; so were Sobel's. But what of Bernard Rayburn?

"The premier is offering you the power—begging you to take it"—Hom's words came back. Quigg and Madelyn had stated the same thing. All logical except for the mindblock. What secret was so great that Rayburn would mindblock him? That was the puzzler.

But Rayburn wanted to see him—convey the offer personally. A place of his own choice, Hom said. Well,

122

Bernard Rayburn would see him; and it would be at a place of his own choice.

Not that he'd tell Hom.

TWELVE

Wehl pushed himself to a sitting position and looked around. In the pale glow of a night lamp, the shadowy outlines of the room took form. Plush chairs, book-lined walls, a corner three-view—winding stairs that led to the master bedroom. The premier's suite!

He felt a wild elation. He'd been able to capture but flickering impressions of the layout of rooms, yet had teleported here unerringly. Perhaps teleportation didn't require an exact knowledge of the goal so much as a desire for the goal itself. And the act was becoming far easier; this time had taken scant seconds.

He rose quietly, his legs so tremulous that he feared they might fail him. The growing weakness of his body brought a desperation he knew he couldn't afford. His eyes went to the winding staircase. He descended them stealthily, paused, and gazed into the shadowy room beyond. The massive bed, the sprawl of furniture, the drapes that covered the glass partition—his memory jumped and danced.

A Guszaco had hung from one wall. He shifted his gaze toward the spot, fastened it on a dark rectangle. He could all but see the sad face of the woman in the painting. I must be Craxton Wehl, he thought despairingly. How else would I have remembered?

He wondered at his own surprise. Despite his acceptance of the role, a small spark of doubt had burned deep in his mind; he had clung to the inner belief that he wasn't Craxton Wehl at all, but was merely a pawn in some gigantic power struggle which involved the real Wehl, Rayburn, and—yes!—Franckel. But how else would he know this suite so well?

He smiled grimly: that made Madelyn his daughter. He'd never quite accepted that. Despite the undeniable physical resemblance, he'd felt no rapport, no feeling of kinship. She'd had the warmth of an ivory statue. But he could still be a pawn! He moved quietly to the drapes, found a button, and pressed it; they slid slowly apart.

The moonlight spilled in, fell in a silver shaft across a sleeping figure on the bed. Wehl moved closer, looking down at the face in the moonwash. He felt a sharp shock. Although undeniably the face of a man in the prime of life, its lines were slack as if the musculature had collapsed. Sunken cheeks gave the effect of a death's-head.

He gazed somberly at the pallid countenance. The man was dying, all right; death was etched into every line of the face. Perhaps he was wrong about Rayburn's motives, he reflected. Certainly a man so near death could have but small ambition. But he had no time for such conjecture.

"Wake up," he said softly. When the figure failed to stir, he reached down and touched a shoulder, then shook it. "Wake up!"

Rayburn groaned, a long, racking groan that filled the room. His body twitched spasmodically. Wehl called his name, shook him again. Abruptly Rayburn's eyes flipped open. For a moment he gazed uncomprehendingly at Wehl's shadowy figure. "Who are you?" he gasped. A hand reached toward a button at the side of the bed, hesitated.

Wehl watched him bemusedly. "You asked to see me." He moved his face into the shaft of moonwash.

"You're Craxton Wehl!"

"So they tell me."

"Thank God," said Rayburn heavily. He pulled himself to a sitting position and rearranged the blankets. "Have you decided to return to Dr. Sundberg's?"

"I'm not convinced that I should."

"What must I do to convince you?" demanded Rayburn.

"Why did you mindblock me?"

"Mindblock? Hom told me about that. It's your imagination, Wehl. You're suffering simple amnesia."

"Not according to the doctor."

"That quack of Quigg's?" Rayburn snorted. "Gerald Sundberg is the top brain specialist in the empire, Wehl.

He *knows* it's amnesia. Didn't your daughter tell you that?"

He nodded reluctantly.

"It's true, Wehl. You had a small tumor removed. You know that, don't you? Sundberg had to go in with the knife. But that's past now. You're as good as new."

"Then why did Madelyn tell me I might die unless I returned to the clinic?" he asked quietly.

"She said that?" Rayburn's head moved up sharply. "It's a possibility, of course. You left before your treatment was completed. Because you did, she's been greatly worried. She's one girl in a million, Wehl. No one has been more anxious for your safe return than she."

"I have one more question."

Rayburn's eyes grew cautious. "Yes?"

"Why did Hom's agent try to kill me?"

Rayburn frowned. "He sold out to the forces that are trying to seize power."

"Franckel?"

"Undoubtedly. Franckel's mad with ambition. If he succeeds, he'll establish a tyranny like the world has never seen. Power-hungry men are dangerous, Wehl. Not that I have to tell you that."

"Is that why I chose you, to prevent Franckel from seizing power?"

"That and to stifle the discontent in the OutSats."

"How's Jupe?"

"Jupe? Oh, the dog." Rayburn's eyes flashed. "You're trying to trick me."

"Why should I try that?"

"Asking about the dog I had on Europa."

"I saw a picture of it," explained Wehl.

"You were checking," Rayburn spat angrily. He slung his feet to the floor and sat on the edge of the bed. The exertion made him wince.

"Why should I be checking?"

"You're paranoid," shouted Rayburn. "Your mind is filled with twists. You have a persecution complex; that's why you consulted Sundberg in the first place. You can't trust anyone, Wehl. You believe everyone is out to get you."

"Isn't that the truth?" He smiled faintly.

Rayburn stiffened. In the pale moonwash Wehl saw him struggle to contain his anger. His big hands clenched and

125

unclenched. With effort, he forced his face into a semblance of calmness. "We're both under tremendous pressure," he said finally. "Let's talk like reasonable men."

"I'll confess that I'm under pressure. I'll also have to admit that I was checking."

"Don't you believe that I'm Bernard Rayburn?"

"I'm not satisfied that anything is as it seems."

"What are you trying to say?"

"I have a mindblock; I know that."

"Ridiculous," Rayburn snorted. "That's part of your persecution complex."

"At first I believed I was Gerald Sundberg. Did you know that? But Felix Quigg, Madelyn, Sundberg's attendant, your Colonel Hom—they all told me that I'm Craxton Wehl, so I must be." He sighed.

"You are," Rayburn affirmed shortly.

"I also didn't believe you are Bernard Rayburn."

"What do you want, my fingerprints, retinal prints? Name it."

"Oh, they'd match."

"You can see how badly you need treatment, Wehl."

"Perhaps." He regarded the other broodingly. "I still have the feeling that I'm the victim of some gigantic conspiracy, or that you are, or that we both are. Did the succession ceremony actually take place?"

Rayburn's head jerked up. "A dozen people witnessed it, including your own daughter."

"I know," he said wearily, "but was I under hypnosis at the time? Were you? Perhaps we're both acting out roles, being manipulated. How do you know that you're dying of Europa fever? Perhaps Sundberg inoculated you with something to pave the way for Franckel."

"I know Europa fever," Rayburn rasped.

"I'm trying to tell you the crazy things that go through my mind," Wehl persisted. "But are they crazy? I don't know. If I'm mindblocked, how do I really know that I'm Craxton Wehl? I know only what I'm told. Do I really know that you're Bernard Rayburn? Who would interpret the fingerprints and retinal pattern? Your men?"

"You're accusing me of tricking you," shouted Rayburn angrily. "It's ridiculous."

"Is it? I don't know."

"You're out of your mind!"

"Then why do you want me back?"

"For the good of the empire, Wehl. I have no recourse."

"Anyone's better than Franckel, is that it?"

Rayburn ignored the point. "You have to return!"

"Have I an alternative?"

"None." The word came as a flat snap.

"I'll come back." Wehl sighed.

"To Sundberg's clinic?"

He nodded. "When you die."

"What?" Rayburn lurched unsteadily to his feet. "That'll be too late."

"You can pass the power to me here," he suggested.

"You have to be cured first!"

"You're dying," he said remorselessly. "There's no time."

"Dying?" Rayburn's hand went involuntarily to his throat. "Yes, I am dying."

"You're as good as dead. Call Hom and whomever it takes and we'll hold the ceremony now."

"No," croaked Rayburn.

"It's for the good of the empire," he reminded.

"Yes, certainly." Rayburn groped for words. "I won't return the power until Sundberg checks you out."

Wehl shook his head decisively. "I won't return to the clinic."

"My God, Wehl, I'm dying. You can grant me that much."

"No," he answered stonily.

"You'd deny that request? Why?"

"Because"—Wehl stared steadily at him—"I'm telepathic. Didn't Hom tell you?"

"Tele ..." Rayburn's jaws worked convulsively. "It's not true," he croaked. "It's part of your trouble— delusions of grandeur."

"Is my teleportation?"

"The surgery caused that!"

"Then why so surprised at the telepathy?" asked Wehl. He held the other's eyes. "Teleportation and telepathy—I have the power."

"You're deluded," Rayburn gasped.

"Would you want a deluded man as a premier?"

"No, no, you can be cured." Rayburn pulled himself

127

together with effort. "I'm distraught, Wehl. All this has been quite a shock. Am I asking too much that I want you to complete your treatment? I have to know that I'm leaving the empire in safe and, yes, sane hands."

"Here or nowhere," he answered implacably.

"For God's sake, Wehl!"

"You forget, I can read your mind."

"No!" Rayburn shouted hoarsely. "You're lying."

"I am?"

"If you could read my mind, you'd return."

"I would?" The belief that Rayburn was dangerously near the cracking edge made Wehl tense and edgy. He frantically groped for a way to push the advantage.

"I hold your life in my hands," shouted Rayburn.

"Perhaps."

"Telepath!" Rayburn laughed wildly. "You're a liar!"

"What is it I don't know?"

"There, you admit that you can't read my mind!"

"Not perfectly."

"I knew you couldn't." Rayburn appeared to draw strength from the assertion. "You have to do as I say. It's your only salvation—the salvation of the empire."

He shook his head. "I've stated my terms."

"Think of the empire!"

"No!"

"Think of Madelyn!"

"You can't sway me," he said wearily.

"You're going back, Wehl!"

"You can't force me."

"I can't?" Rayburn's face, in the moonwash, was quivering with emotion. "I hold your life in my palm—I told you that! Go back or die!"

"You'd kill me?" Wehl suppressed his shock. Clearly the other's concern was not for the empire. His stake was personal; his words fairly shouted that. If that were true, Rayburn couldn't be dying; the whole affair must be a ghastly trick. Briefly he wondered if Rayburn weren't right; perhaps he was demented! Perhaps he was tilting with phantoms in an illusory world that didn't exist beyond the confines of his disordered mind.

He violently rejected the thought. Lord, if only he could read Rayburn's mind! It was apparent the man was dying; it was etched into the gaunt face. The muscles of the big

128

body were so slack the man scarcely could support himself.

Then why did Rayburn insist that he return to Sundberg? The question screamed in his mind, left him weak and empty. If the purpose were to kill him, Hom could have accomplished that readily enough. Somehow everything was tied in with the mindblock—some terrible secret that he had possessed and was made to forget. Or was Rayburn, like himself, a puppet?

Perhaps Rayburn actually didn't know about the mindblock! The thought jolted him. Was Sundberg the Machiavelli? Or was he, in turn, the pawn of a stronger power? Oh God! He pressed his fingertips to his temples.

"You'll die," screamed Rayburn.

"Not until I know the truth," he gasped.

"You fool, you'll kill us both!"

"Then for God's sake, talk!"

"I offer you life, Wehl. Isn't that enough?"

"At what price?"

"Return to Sundberg's!"

"Talk, damn you!" Wehl stared at him, wishing desperately that he could read his mind—baffled that he couldn't. For an instant he had the impression of a chaotic jumble of thoughts hedged in by fear and desperation. Rayburn's mind, or his own? "You haven't much time," he shouted.

"You'll die with me," gasped Rayburn.

"Not till I know the full truth about myself," he cried. "Give me back my memories, Rayburn!"

"Only Sundberg can do that!"

"I'll see Sundberg on my own terms!" he yelled. "I'll squeeze it out of him, Rayburn, and to hell with the power. I'm on my way."

"Don't go," Rayburn screamed. He lurched toward Wehl, stumbled, then pulled himself slowly erect. Fear twisted his features into a grotesque mask. He commenced to sway, fought to steady himself, toppled suddenly facedown to the floor.

Wehl leaped to his side and rolled him over. The exertion left him gasping. He frantically felt for Rayburn's pulse, found it; the beat was weak under his finger. Weak and sporadic. He placed an ear to the premier's broad chest; the heartbeat came like the wild flutter of wings.

129

His brow was cold, clammy. Wehl struggled erect. Rayburn couldn't die! Not till he talked! He ran to the door and flung it open.

A guard jerked to attention, then gaped bewilderly. "Who are you?" he demanded.

"Quick, get a doctor!"

"Not until . . . My God, you're Mr. Wehl!"

"Quick, man, the premier's dying!"

"Yes, sir, the doctor's in the guest quarters." As the guard sped away, Wehl returned inside and turned on the lights. Sprawled alongside the bed, Rayburn's big body resembled a chunk of gray clay. Only the sporadic rise and fall of his chest and the bubbly exhalation that flecked his lips told of life.

He gazed at the premier's gaunt face. Were it not for the slackness of the muscles, the dark hollows under the eyes, the face would be strong and lean. As it was, it held a dissolute quality—the face of death, he thought. The hands and feet protruding out from the nightclothes held an alabaster paleness.

"What's in your mind?" he whispered. He closed his eyes despairingly. If telepathy were like teleportation, it should be subject to his will. But it wasn't; that was the damnable part. Oh, he sensed things, like the presence of people—or had on a few occasions—but the real power eluded him. Perhaps, like Obie Frye, he was a partial, or a partial partial. The thought brought a wince.

He gazed at Rayburn with the hollow feeling that should the man die his own fate was sealed. He pushed the panicky feeling aside; it wasn't death that he feared, but the anonymity of his being. *Who am I?* The dying man at his feet knew.

Movement from beyond the door brought him around. A thin, bony figure in a dressing gown entered hurriedly. A black satchel identified him as the doctor. He glanced at Wehl, jerked back his head. "Craxton Wehl!" he exclaimed.

"Then you must be . . ." Wehl's heart began to thump.

"Gerald Sundberg, the premier's physician. And yours," he added primly.

"You'd better take a look at him." Wehl gestured toward the figure on the floor. "I think he's going."

"You'd better hope you're wrong."

130

"Why?" he challenged.

Sundberg didn't answer. Bending over the unconscious man, he took his pulse, listened to his heart, lifted an eyelid, and watched it slide back over the glazed orb. Finally he straightened. "We'll have to get him to the clinic fast."

"Will he make it?" Wehl felt edgy.

"I wouldn't vouch for it." Sundberg gave brisk orders to the guard, then turned back, his face speculative. "You left my care rather abruptly, Mr. Wehl. It's imperative that you return immediately."

"It is?" Wehl restrained his ire.

"You're a sick man."

"Mindblocked," snapped Wehl. "Why did you do it?"

Sundberg looked shaken. "You're laboring under a delusion," he said. "Amnesia, yes, but nothing that won't respond to treatment."

"Why did Rayburn say I was as good as dead if I didn't return?"

"Rayburn said that?" Sundberg's head jerked convulsively.

"So did Madelyn and your attendant, Kelsey."

"It's not true," cried Sundberg.

"What is the truth?" he demanded. Sundberg's jaw muscles twitched nervously. He darted a glance toward the door. Wehl sensed the panic in the medic's mind. "Talk," he gritted harshly.

"It's better that you don't know," blurted Sundberg.

"I'll be the judge of that."

Sundberg straightened with visible effort. "For your sake, no."

Wehl gestured toward the figure on the floor. "Is that man Bernard Rayburn?"

"Yes, certainly." Sundberg's face took on an ashen hue.

"Am I Craxton Wehl?"

"Your own daughter identified you."

"Answer me," he shouted.

"Yes, certainly you are Craxton Wehl." Sundberg attempted to muster his dignity. "I've been your physician for over fifteen years, Wehl. I've been privy to every thought you've ever had. Why would I lie to you?"

"You are lying!" Wehl fought to suppress the emotion that surged in his vitals. He had to break Sundberg! He

131

held the other's gaze, waiting for it to waver. When it didn't, he said, "You know I'm a teleport, Sundberg. Do you know I'm telepathic?"

"No!" The denial came with a strangled cry.

"I'm reading you, Sundberg!"

"You can't be! If you were, you wouldn't have asked the questions you did."

"I haven't total power but enough," he pursued relentlessly. "I know you tricked me."

"On my honor, Wehl."

"You're lying, Sundberg!"

"No! No!"

"When I return to power, you go to Pluto!"

"Oh?" Sundberg's face grew suddenly still. "You can't frighten me."

"You don't believe I'll get the power?"

"If you complete your cure, yes. That's Rayburn's expressed wish."

"I'll have you Pluto-bound before the week's out," Wehl cried hoarsely. Sundberg's sudden calm baffled him. "You'll never see the sun again! You'll live in eternal night! You'll live in a burrow like an animal—never see the stars except through a dismal dome. Staring at the sky through a dome. The sky, the sky . . ."

He clutched at his throat, swayed weakly. *The distorted sky!* My God . . .

"Pull yourself together, man!" Sundberg's words came as if from across a great void.

"No trees, no flowers, no grass," he gasped. "Nothing but masses of frozen methane and ammonia whirling under an alien sky. You won't live long out there; people don't."

"Here, let me give you a sedative." Sundberg grasped his arm.

"No!" He jerked it free and stepped back, then shook his head to clear it. Sundberg's face came into focus. "The truth, tell me the truth," he shouted.

"Please, listen!"

"The truth, damn you! I'm peeping you!"

"I'm trying to protect you, Wehl."

"From what?"

"From yourself!"

"Myself?" He felt a shock.

"You haven't completed your treatment, Wehl. Your

mind is disintegrating. You're paranoid; you believe everyone is conspiring against you. The world is your enemy. It started years ago—became worse and worse until you were living in a world of complete delusion. You trusted no one. You began plotting against mythical plotters . . ."

"You're saying I'm crazy," he cried.

"Sick," Sundberg reprimanded. "You broke physically and mentally. When the situation became dangerous to the state, you were spirited to my clinic to keep you from public view. Did you know that your own daughter arranged that? She realized that something had to be done."

"My daughter?" he asked numbly.

"For the good of the state," affirmed Sundberg.

"Where does Rayburn fit into this?" he asked bewilderedly.

"The governers were growing uneasy, Wehl. You brought him here before you were committed to still the outcry for your retirement. You never intended to pass him the power."

"Did I?"

"In one of your more lucid moments, yes. Madelyn persuaded you."

"You said I was power-mad!"

"Completely," Sundberg agreed.

"If that were so, would I have given him the power? Not if I were as mentally deranged as you say; especially not in a lucid moment. You're lying!"

Sundberg shifted uneasily. "There's more to it," he admitted.

"What?"

"I put you under hypnosis, planted the suggestion. That was on your daughter's counsel," he added hurriedly.

"You tricked me," Wehl raged.

"For the good of the empire, yes. When you're fully recovered, I'm confident you'll admit that." Sundberg smiled professionally. "Shortly afterward I discovered a tumor, removed it. We hold every hope for your complete recovery—contingent upon continuing your treatment, of course."

"My God, I'm crazy!"

"It's not too late, Wehl."

"You can cure me?" he asked desperately.

"Yes, but there's not much time."

"I forgot!"

"Forgot what?" Sundberg arched his eyes.

"You mindblocked me!"

"I'll admit it."

"You admit it?" Wehl stared askance at him. "Why did you do it?" he cried.

"To make you forget the twisted creature you'd become. That's what Madelyn and Rayburn were trying to protect you from, Wehl—the shock of knowing what you were. Do you realize you even tried to poison Madelyn?"

"My own daughter?" He groaned. "No wonder you wouldn't tell me."

"You believed she was plotting against you," explained Sundberg. "Perhaps it's good therapy for you to know the worst. Do you know why Rayburn's dying?"

"Europa fever," he shouted. "You said so yourself!"

"Administered by inoculation, Wehl. You arranged that when you realized you'd passed the power. You couldn't allow your successor to live; your ego was too great to admit that you could be succeeded. You did that, Wehl."

"I . . . did that?" His eyes were pleading. "Does Rayburn know?"

"The burden of that knowledge is mine," said Sundberg, "and yours."

"I'm a monster," he sobbed.

"It's not too late, Wehl. The recognition of what you were—your sheer abhorrence of it—proves that the surgery removed the cause. A man can't be condemned for a biological causation, Wehl; the law has recognized that since ancient times."

"I'm a murderer!"

"You're well on the road to recovery," rebutted Sundberg. "A bit of therapy, then you can make amends by taking back the power—governing as the wise and just man you were before your illness."

"I can't, I can't. I couldn't live with that on my conscience." He buried his face in his hands.

"Oh, I'll block it out."

"You'll what?" Wehl's head bobbed up.

"Block it out. You won't remember."

"My God, you can remake a man's life, can't you?" Wehl stared at him, aghast. "You can shape his actions through hypnosis, blot out his past. I'm a murderer and you offer to erase it from my memory, as if that made the matter all right. But what of Bernard Rayburn? Would it be all right with him? Who's the monster, Sundberg, you or I?"

"It was necessary," Sundberg snapped stiffly.

"What else did you blot out, tell me that? What other influences did you implant in my mind? Which of us is the real killer, Sundberg? Tell me that!"

"Quiet," the medic hissed. He threw a nervous glance toward the entrance to the room.

"I'll tell the world, I'll tell the universe," shouted Wehl. He laughed, a mocking note that echoed in the corridor. The guard's frightened face was visible at the door.

"You need a sedative," Sundberg cried hoarsely. He fumbled in his bag.

"I need the truth!" yelled Wehl. "Who am I, Sundberg, man or monster? Or am I a damned puppet, dancing on your string? Do you know what I'll do if I get the power? I'll throw you out of the universe!"

"Quiet," hissed Sundberg again.

"The quiet man! No more, Sundberg!" He heard a noise at the door and whirled as two men hurried in bearing a stretcher. Movement in the periphery of his eye brought him back around as Sundberg lunged swiftly toward him, a hypodermic syringe in his hand. Wehl propelled himself backward. "Too late," he croaked.

As Sundberg's hand snaked out with the needle, he teleported.

THIRTEEN

"I'm Craxton Wehl, all right," he told Mura. "I must be; everyone's story is the same. Rayburn's dying, needs me back to prevent a political upheaval. Sundberg even admitted the mindblock."

"He did?" She showed her surprise. "Did he explain it?"

"To make me forget how twisted I'd become," he replied bitterly. He told her what the medic had said.

"I can't believe that," she exclaimed.

"That I'd try to poison my own daughter or arrange my successor's death?" He smiled faintly. "You said yourself that I was whispered to be crazy, warped—a tyrant."

"But that was before I knew who you were," she protested. Her face flamed.

"What difference does that make?"

"I know you now; you're not like that at all. Besides, there was the tumor. Oh, you can't condemn yourself. You have to take yourself as you are, not as you were."

"You believe I should return to the clinic?"

"I . . . don't know."

"You have doubts," he accused.

"It's all so mixed up. I don't know what to believe."

"I know, I have my own doubts, perhaps because of the snatches of memory that I never can quite pin down. Like Mr. Krant's candy store."

"There was a Krant's candy shop on the corner years ago," she said in a hushed voice. "I checked."

"So did I."

"What does that mean?"

"I keep asking myself the same question," he answered. "I was born in Rochester—the New York megalopolis. I looked it up in the library. I was mayor, governor of the Americas, didn't come here until I succeeded to the Big Power Seat. So how could I know about Krant's candy store?" He eyed her perplexedly.

"I don't know," she whispered.

"There are other memories—like the tower at the space terminal. I can see the aircars flitting like silver moths through the beacon at night, but it's a memory of long ago—more like an echo in the mind," he added.

"I have old memories like that." She glanced away, her face troubled.

"I felt the ping of memory at the first sight of this room," he continued. "It was as if something were knocking at the door to my subconscious. Of all the tens of millions of rooms in the city, why did I teleport to this particular one? I feel the same whenever I walk along Glade Avenue—a curious nostalgia. But how can one be nostalgic for something he has never known? And, oh!" He sat straighter.

"What is it?" she asked worriedly.

"I had a vision while I was talking with Rayburn. The distorted sky—I saw it again."

"Oh?" Her lips formed a small circle. "You mentioned it that night at Obie Frye's."

"I did? Did I tell you what it's like?" Rushing on, he described the nightmares of the fish eye, of the twisted stars, of the huge blob that rushed in to erase the universe. "Or is that all fantasy?" he ended.

"Fish eye?" She looked wonderingly at him. "The miniature domes."

"I don't follow you," he confessed.

"That's what we call the miniature domes on Mars." Seeing his perplexity, she explained how the first colonists used to flock to the domes at night to watch the stars. But as the atomic disintegrators carved more and more caverns and the town grew, the big domes became inadequate to accommodate the crowds. Others lived too far away to visit them. As a result, many people developed claustrophobia; some went mad. To correct the situation, the engineers bored shafts upward through the rock along all the tunnels, capping them with miniature domes. Now such domes were strewn throughout the underground world.

"I used to run up the spiral stairs to watch the stars at night," she exclaimed. Her eyes glistened.

"Like looking upward through the bottom of a bowl?" he asked tensely.

"It had that effect—distortion." She nodded. "Perhaps that's why they likened them to fish eyes. They had the same bulbous appearance."

"But the universe—what blots out the universe?"

"I don't know," she whispered. "Have you ever been to Mars?"

"Perhaps as premier. How would I know?"

"It would have been long ago, else I would have remembered it."

"Lord, the memories haunt me."

"All that will pass," she encouraged.

"Will it? I'm not so certain."

"You can't let yourself think that way," she chided. Her eyes grew questioning. "Did you try to peep them?"

137

"Rayburn and Sundberg both," he acquiesced. "It didn't work."

"You once thought . . ."

"That I was telepathic? Yes, I'm still not certain."

"Perhaps it's still developing."

"Possibly, I don't know."

"Try to read my mind," she commanded.

"I couldn't do that!"

"Try," she urged. "You have to know."

"I'll try a stranger on the street first, not you."

"I have nothing to hide."

"I know that, but you might never feel the same again."

"What color am I thinking of?" she asked quickly.

"Purple."

Awe-struck, she gazed at him. "That was it," she whispered.

"A guess." He laughed. "I named the first color that came to mind."

"Did you, or were you reading mine?"

"No, I guessed." Even as he spoke, he wondered why that particular color had come so readily to mind. Certainly it wasn't outstanding in the hierarchy of colors one usually thought of.

"You don't believe that," she insisted.

"I don't know."

"Try again."

Reluctantly he brought his eyes to her face. Once he had thought it rather plain; now he was captured by the symmetry of her features, the almost exquisite lines that molded her nose and lips. Strange, he'd never noticed that her eyes held a touch of green—like the sun-struck waters of a tropic beach, he thought.

Then, suddenly, for the first time in his memory he found himself gazing into the immense citadel of another human mind. He had the immediate sense of great strength, a calmness, a compassion that flowed outward to him, touching him as gently as a summer breeze. Startled at the imagery that began to form, he quickly withdrew.

"You saw," she whispered. He nodded uncomfortably; such an invasion should never be. She stated, "You are telepathic. You have but to find the key."

He rose and went to the window, gazing at the distant tower of the space terminal. In his mind it seemed that he had known it for all the years of his life—slender, musty-colored, an ancient finger pointing at the stars. Like himself, he thought wistfully, it was from another age.

He had the power! If it were developing, as Mura had suggested, how far might it develop? Normally he would have considered teleportation the furthest reach of such talents, even beyond psychokinesis and clairvoyance. Telepathy more logically would appear as a first step—a notch or two above intuition.

Clairvoyance—the word came back, startling him. *He'd seen Kelsey in his quarters reading!* He'd had a stark mental picture, only he hadn't realized it at the time. He'd attributed it to surmise.

His hands trembled. The power was there, if only he knew how to trigger it. Telepathy and clairvoyance—discover the key and he'd put Quigg and Hom and Sundberg through the wringer, discover once and for all the answers to the engima which enveloped him. Would he like to look into Madelyn's mind? He found the prospect distasteful.

He became aware that Mura was watching him. She's troubled, he thought. He felt a pang of guilt at the turmoil he'd brought into her life, yet was extremely grateful to her. Perhaps he could make it up to her some day. He jerked erect, the hair at the nape of his neck tingling. Two aircars flashed through his visual field, dropping to the street below. A startled exclamation escaped his lips.

"What is it?" Mura sprang from the couch.

"A raid!" He gazed hypnotically at the uniformed figures spilling from the vehicles, then whirled toward her. "Get out of here," he cried.

"They're after you," she exclaimed.

"Run, girl! Wait, perhaps we can get out the back way!" He raced to the end of the hall and looked out the rear window. Another aircar blocked the back entrance. Movement overhead caused him to jerk his gaze upward: a fourth vehicle was descending toward the roof. He whirled and ran back to the room. "Quick, hide in one of the other apartments," he cried.

"They want you, not me!" Her face was frightened.

"Hurry," he begged. Her face blanched at the sound of feet pounding up the stairwell.

"Teleport," she screamed.

"Not without you!"

"They don't want me!"

"I won't leave you here," he cried.

"Hurry or they'll kill you," she shrieked. A crashing came at the door. "Please," she begged.

"Mura . . ."

"Hurry!"

"I'll come back," he promised.

"Teleport!" she screamed.

Teleport! Teleport! To where? Was this a trick to stampede him into fleeing to the sky clinic? *Teleport, teleport, teleport . . .* Dimly he heard the door splinter, crash inward; he had the faraway impression of uniformed figures bursting into the room.

"Stand where you are!" a voice roared.

Instant blackness came.

In what seemed the blink of an eye Wehl found himself sprawled on the concrete, his eyes blinded by the blaze of the sun.

"He came out of nowhere!" a woman screamed. He scrambled to his feet and looked around. Several startled men and woman were watching him, their faces frightened. He glimpsed a small island formed by a moat, the mechanical pigeons. Craxton Wehl Park!

The woman screamed again. As he stumbled blindly away, he saw a cop racing toward him. He looked wildly around for a means of escape.

"Hey, you!" the cop shouted. Wehl started to run, conscious that his legs, weak and rubbery, threatened to buckle under him. He plunged desperately toward the shrubbery lining the walk.

"Halt!" the cop thundered. The command struck him like a blast. The fear surging through him, he propelled himself toward the cover of the bushes. *Escape! Escape!* The word rang in his mind. *He had to teleport!* He scarcely glimpsed the wall of the blackness into which he plunged headlong.

A shriek rang in his ears.

He clambered to his feet. Dirty gray walls, a narrow cot, a barred window—the bloated, fear-filled face of a derelict, hands clutched at his throat. The man's eyes held sheer panic. Abruptly he whirled, clawed at the bars.

"Let me out, let me out!" he screamed. "I'm going

140

crazy!" Wehl stared incredulously at him. My God, he was back in jail! As he backed away from the screaming man, feet pounded in the passageway, then the turnkey was gaping at him through the grille.

"How'd you get in there?" he roared.

"Let me out!" the derelict screamed. Wehl stared hypnotically at him, his mind in turmoil. Anywhere but here, he thought desperately. Anywhere! Anywhere! *He had to teleport!* The jailer's hand snaked out with a bunch of keys; one grated in the lock and the steel door creaked open. The jailer's form filled the entrance.

"Wise guy," he snarled.

Wehl teleported.

He struggled erect, staring across an ornate desk into Felix Quigg's startled face. It struck him that he'd never been in Quigg's private office before. Then how . . . ?

Quigg lurched into instant action. Wehl saw a hand dart toward a drawer, sweep up with a stun gun. The barrel swung . . .

He teleported.

Obie Frye, petrified with fright, stared at him from across a dirty room. The peeper's mouth worked convulsively. Obie Frye! Wehl felt a stab of jubilation. He'd make him talk, force him.

"No!" The word exploded from Frye's lips as he bolted toward the door. He jerked it open and raced screaming into the hall. As his cries floated back, other doors began to open. Chagrined, Wehl realized Frye must have read the violence in his mind. Sensing the growing confusion in the hall, he teleported.

He stared upward at a white ceiling, only dimly aware of a tube that ran from one arm to a liquid-filled bottle suspended above the bed. The strong odor of disinfectant filled his nostrils. *Where am I?* The question came dreamily.

Blurred movement in the periphery of one eye caught his attention and he swiveled his head; the pain was excruciating. Appearing afloat in a sea of mist, phantom eyes watched him from above gauze masks. One, two, three pairs of eyes.

"Who are you?" he screamed.

"He's out of his head," a voice said.

"Quiet, he's coming out of it."

141

"My God, he's ..."

"Shhhh!"

The faces above the white masks steadied, sharpened, took form. Gerald Sundberg, Kelsey, the young nurse!

"No! No!" he screamed.

"Quiet, Mr. Wehl," Sundberg ordered crisply.

"I'm not Wehl! I'm not! I'm not!" Stark terror swirled through him. Why did they say he was Wehl? He tried to struggle erect, found he was strapped to the table. The room was growing dark. He ...

... flipped open his eyes, staring upward into a rack of suits. A young man with a frightened face was gaping at him. He scrambled sheepishly to his feet. "Where am I?"

"Martin's Men's Shop," the other stammered.

"Martin's?" The name held a familiar ring. An older man ran toward him from behind a counter.

"Where'd you come from?" he demanded suspiciously.

"Martin's?" Wehl repeated. His memory clicked. The older man was the manager of ... "I was here several days ago asking you about Krant's candy store."

"Krant's? Yes, but ..."

"When was Krant here?" he cut in.

"Well, I can't ..."

"When, man, when?"

"Eighteen or twenty years ago," the other managed to say.

"You're certain of that?" Wehl grasped his arm, shook it.

"Let me go!" The manager wrenched his arm free and leaped back.

"I have to be certain," he said desperately. "Look at me man, I'm Craxton Wehl!"

"He's crazy," the manager shouted. "Call the police!"

"Yes, sir." The younger man raced from the store.

"How long, how long?" Wehl cried.

"Eighteen or twenty, I told you." The manager fled to the rear of the store.

"Police! Police! A crazy man!" The words floated in from the street.

Wehl teleported.

The universe reeled.

He was falling, tumbling through the black canyons of the sky. The stars were chaotic streaks of light. The sun,

142

an intolerably brilliant disc pasted against the nigrescent night, grew smaller and smaller and smaller until it was lost in the splay of light thrown out by madly spinning galaxies.

Dream or reality—which was which? Could a dream come disguised as reality, or reality as a dream? Where in the spinning vastness around him was the real world? What was time and what was space? What was the nature of matter?

He drifted in amorphic blackness in which past and present and future were as one. Time was timeless. He tried to stir his muscles, had the impression that no body existed; he was pure thought, a wanderer in a wasteland of such magnitude that its borders were incomprehensible.

Dimly he remembered the apartment, the raid. All that seemed long ago. From what past had the memory come? But the raiders couldn't have hoped to catch him, he reflected dreamily. Not a teleport. So why the raid? He drifted, drifted, drifted.

Mura! The name pinged in his consciousness. They weren't after him; they were after her. They were getting at him through her. Hom—that would be Hom.

Mura! Mura! He projected the name out into the sweep of infinity. No answer came. Where was she? He tried again to sense the physical part of him that he remembered, and failed. Somehow he was out of contact with . . . himself! The quiet, the peace . . .

Craxton Wehl Park, the jail, Felix Quigg's reach for the stun gun, Obie Frye's panicky flight—the memories came in the masks of dreams. Sundberg's clinic! Sundberg watching him from above the gauze mask. That had been . . . when? That had been in then-time, not now-time.

Then-time, now-time; he puzzled over it. Time had dimensions, of course, but how could he have gone from now-time to then-time? The park, the jail, Quigg, Obie Frye, and Martin's Men's Shop had all been in now-time; but not his reappearance in the clinic.

Dreamily he grappled with the problem. He had gone back through time, reemerging once again through the postoperative stage; he had gone back to awaken from the brain surgery. Had he lived that scene twice, or had he relived it only in the hidden corridors of his mind?

Krant's candy shop! He felt a stir of puzzlement.

Krant's candy shop had existed in his childhood, had been buried under an avalanche of years. Only it hadn't; it had existed a scant eighteen or twenty years ago. He'd been premier at the time, so how could he have visited it? Yet he had. He could fairly sniff the delicious aroma of hot chocolate; and he'd been young. What warps had time? None of it made sense, he thought wearily. Perhaps it was all a mad, mad dream.

He drifted, drifted, drifted. Then abruptly the stars steadied, blazed down with a cold, brittle light.

The fish eye!
The distorted sky!
He stood under a small cupola that curved down on all sides of him, gazed upward into a black night alive with fantastic burning suns. Their rays, caught in the curvature of the dome, refracted and splintered into odd geometrical forms. He tried to tear his eyes from their harsh light, but couldn't; he was paralyzed. The stars screamed! A gigantic spheroid, flattened at the poles, edged into view; one by one it blotted out the flaming suns.
The blob! The blob! The . . .

"*Aaaugh!*"

He awoke, the scream on his lips. Fright swirled through his mind. He pushed himself to a sitting position and looked around frantically. The shabby couch, the table with the artificial flowers . . . Mura's apartment!

He struggled to his feet, his visions flooding back. The dome, a bulging fish eye through which he'd gazed into the primeval seas of space! The distorted sky, just as Mura had described it! He'd seen it! He'd seen it! How could that be? But he had; and the blob! Oh God, the twists and warps of the mind! Had he batted back and forth through time and space, or had he pierced through to the blocked-off banks of his memory?

Krant's candy store! Eighteen or twenty years ago, the man had said. He groaned aloud. The time-scale was all awry. How could he put the years in order, draw a time-line that made sense? He couldn't if he accepted himself as he was.

144

He groped with his thoughts. What was memory but the mental replica of things known or experienced. He'd lived those years! He'd smelt the aroma of hot chocolate; and he'd been young! He'd take that as a starter. What did that do to the time-line?

The familiarity of Glade Avenue, Mr. Krant, the distorted sky—he let the memories tumble like drops, one by one through his mind. How could his youth have coincided with the existence of the candy store? How could he have looked up through the fish eye of an alien world? What was the blob that ate the stars?

The blob! He swayed, pictured the monstrous mass that gobbled its way through the universe. *Memory is the replica of things known or experienced!* The blob was . . .

He lurched upright, trembling violently at the monstrous thought that struck him. It seemed absolutely inconceivable; but was it? He tried to sort through the facts to meet this new surmise. *The premier was dying of Europa fever!* Item one. Only Kelsey, who had attended him, hadn't known the symptoms of the disease. *And he was dying.* Item two. Kelsey, Madelyn—they'd all told him that. Now Rayburn had to return the power. He pulled his jumbled thoughts together. If he were right, the reason for his mindblock was abundantly clear.

"Dear God, no," he whispered violently; but with a terrible sickness of the soul, he knew he'd found the truth. *He knew!* It fitted the time-line perfectly! He'd been tricked, cheated of his heritage, robbed of his past and future. They'd all conspired against him! And the premier was the master conspirator of them all. Only he wasn't the premier!

He was an impostor!

Mura! Memory of the raid rushed back. He looked around frantically. Sight of a toppled chair and the splintered door brought the clutch of fear to his throat. "Mura," he called hoarsely. Although the silence told him he was alone, he ran to her door and pounded against it. When no answer came, he twisted the knob and entered.

Gone! He gazed in anguish at the deserted room, then recoiled at the sight of a new radiophone installed on a stand in one corner. He took a step backward, the fear unfolding in his mind. *The phone was for him!* The knowledge struck him like a physical blow. They'd kidnaped

Mura and now were prepared to deal with him on their own terms. A consuming anger gripped him. *Mr. Krant, the fish eye, the blob that ate the stars*—those things changed the terms, only they didn't know that.

But he knew. Too late? A sudden calm gripped him. He had a chance, a slim chance. But he had to trust Hom! The hope brought a swirl of excitement. He sidled to a chair and sat, his eyes on the instrument.

After a moment it rang.

FOURTEEN

As the small screen on the radiophone glowed to life, Madelyn Wehl's face took form. It held a cool, imperious look. Wehl suppressed a distinct shock; he'd felt certain his caller would be Hom.

"Father!" Her face creased into a glossy smile.

"Where's Mura?" he demanded.

"Safe."

"What have you done with her?" His hands shook as he tried to restrain his anger.

"Please," she pouted, "we're getting nowhere this way. Isn't it sufficient that you know she's safe?"

"I don't know that," he shouted.

"She's under the protection of my private police."

"How'd you know where I was?"

"Oh, I hired Quigg and Associates. They're very good at that sort of thing."

"It'll serve you right when he sells you out," he exclaimed bitterly.

"He can't. I have him under total contract for the month." She attempted another smile. "All I ask is your safe return."

"State your terms," he said coldly. "I know you have them."

"The girl will be released when you return to Sundberg's clinic."

146

"If I refuse?"

"She goes to Pluto."

"What?" He stared incredulously at her. "You'd do that?"

"For your own good, yes."

He started to burst out with the horrible truth at which he'd arrived, then restrained himself. Time enough for that. Instead he said, "You'll have to give me time."

"There's no time left," she replied crisply. "The premier's at the point of death."

"A day," he pleaded.

"No."

"An hour!"

"No. I'm on my way to pick you up, return you. If you're not ready, the girl goes to Pluto." The screen went dark. He gazed helplessly at it. He had thirty minutes, if that. And she'd carry out the threat. She'd do it even if he did return, he thought desperately. She was that vindictive. But she was right; time was running out.

Hastily he called Information Central and put through a call. The screen came to life to the raucous sound of Martian nose flutes. A green and orange sign gave a pitch for Felix Quigg & Associates. The sign was replaced by the face of a blonde young woman with a professional smile. "May I help you?" she asked.

"Get me Felix Quigg."

"I'm sorry but . . ."

"This is Craxton Wehl," he cut in irritably.

"Oh, Mr. Wehl!" She tried to conceal her shock. "Yes, certainly, I'll see if he's in." The screen went blank. Within seconds it lighted up again and Felix Quigg's narrow face came on.

Wehl snapped, "Madelyn has kidnaped Mura Breen. Where is she?"

"Oh?" Quigg's tone was wary.

"You arranged it. She told me."

"Please!" Quigg looked pained. "Kidnaping could cost me my license plus a twelve-month suspension of my charge plate. You certainly don't believe . . ."

"Where is she?" he shouted irritably.

"Sorry, Wehl, but I'm under contract for the entire month. The terms prohibit me from . . ."

"Fifty thousand for the information," he cut in.

147

"You have a charge plate?" Quigg's eyes grew calculating.

"Backed by the empire," he stated stiffly.

"Explain that."

"I've decided to return, take back the power."

"You're returning?" The dismay in Quigg's face held a touch of fear. "That's wonderful news."

"Is it?" he asked drily.

"Of a certainty, Mr. Wehl. I'll be happy to help you. There'll be no charge, of course. I seldom do for a public service."

"Where's Miss Breen?"

"Aboard the *Far Horizon*."

"Pluto-bound?"

"I believe it does touch down there, yes."

"You delivered her there," Wehl grated. "You should know."

"I did not," Quigg denied. "That would constitute an illegality punishable by . . ."

"Where did you take her?" he interrupted.

"Wehl House."

"Then how do you know she's aboard the *Far Horizon*?"

Quigg momentarily was flustered. "I was accompanied by my assistant," he explained lamely.

"Well?"

"A peeper."

"Obie Frye?"

"Of course, you've met him—a most discreet person." Quigg frowned. "The information was glimpsed quite unintentionally, of course."

Wehl said, "I have a job for you. You're going to get Miss Breen off that ship, return her to this apartment."

"Impossible!"

"Is it? How would you like to make that trip, Quigg?"

"Pluto? You're joking!" Quigg's jaw muscles convulsed.

"Review my past record," Wehl said coldly. "Is it that of a joker?"

"A distinguished record," Quigg blurted. "I'll do what I can."

"You have"—Wehl glanced at the time—"less than thirty minutes to get her here."

"Less than thirty minutes!" Quigg was aghast. "That's impossible."

"Try bribery," he snapped. "That usually works." He punched a button and watched Quigg's discomfited visage fade from the screen. The sight brought a savage satisfaction. Quigg would manage the job, all right. He knew that with certainty. Still, he couldn't take a chance.

He sat back to reflect on his situation. He was the answer man, at least if his surmise were true. To what avail? He still was caught. But he wasn't beat, not totally. They could never be certain of him until he acquiesced completely. That gave him bargaining power. He might buy Mura's safety; he couldn't hope for much more. He looked at the clock; the minutes were passing swiftly.

He had to return to Sundberg's!

No matter how he played it, he had to go back. The knowledge brought a cold sweat. He'd be doing exactly as they wanted him to. Exactly! And the plan for him was death! That was as certain as the stars in their courses. *The distorted sky!* He wondered if he would ever see it again.

If he could convince Hom . . . He had to, he thought desperately. He had to place his life in the agent's hands. He tapped into Information Central again, spoke briefly. Several faces flickered successively on the screen as his call was put through, then the agent's face formed in front of him.

"It is good to see you, Mr. Wehl," said Hom.

"No doubt," he answered drily. "I've decided to return."

"I'm relieved. The premier is at the point of death."

"There's one condition. Several," he corrected. As he spoke, his scalp prickled—an alarm clanged in his brain. He jerked erect.

"What's wrong?" asked Hom tautly.

"Someone's coming!" He cocked his head, listened, looked at the closed door. The apartment was deserted; he knew that. The alarm came again, a harsh scream in his brain. He had the momentary impression of an aircar on the roof—of a burly, dark-faced man who walked with the tread of a cat. The face faded, came back more strongly than ever. A slash crossed one cheek, twisted the mouth slightly awry.

"The scar-faced man," he blurted.

"Sobel?"

149

"The man who . . ."

"Teleport, get out of there," Hom broke in. He shouted an order over his shoulder.

"I can't," gasped Wehl. "Quigg will be . . ."

"Where's Sobel?" interrupted Hom.

"On the roof. He came by aircar."

"Roof?"

"Clairvoyance—I can see him," he explained. The revelation startled him.

"Teleport, Wehl!"

"No, listen," he pleaded. "Madelyn's private police kidnaped Miss Breen." The words tumbled out. "They have her aboard the *Far Horizon*."

"The Pluto transport?"

"Madelyn threatens to send her there unless I return. I hired Felix Quigg . . ."

"What about Sobel?" Hom cut in.

"He's starting down."

"Teleport, Wehl. Don't delay."

"I can't," he shouted desperately. Thought of what Sobel might do if Mura returned made him panicky. He poured out his fears.

"He's a killer," Hom rasped. "I'll take care of the girl."

"I won't leave until I know she's safe," he cried. Hom cursed and the screen went blank. The danger signal screamed in Wehl's brain again, louder than before. Sobel was quietly descending the stairs. The vision came through so starkly clear that Wehl thought he must be staring directly at the man.

He jerked back his attention, then ran to the door and locked it. The act gave him scant satisfaction. One blast and the door would disintegrate into atoms. He yanked the stun gun from his pocket. Perhaps he could bluff Sobel, delay him long enough to get a shot at him. The realization that this time Sobel would be prepared brought a sick feeling; he couldn't hope to trick the man as he had aboard the sky clinic.

Teleport! The word dinned in his consciousness. He couldn't, not with the possibility that Quigg might return with Mura. His attention focused on the door, he tried to locate the agent. He had the impression of the big body again, the soft step; the vision came into focus.

Perhaps the old man's asleep. The thought ran through

150

Wehl's mind like a whisper borne by the wind. He struggled to grasp its meaning, then realized he'd reached Sobel's mind. Telepathy! The knowledge staggered him. Somehow, in some way, he'd found the key! Perhaps that's what was needed—the survival factor! The excitement pounded at his temples.

He attempted to reach out, catch the visual Sobel with the camera of his mind. Sobel's image flared and ebbed, flared again. Wehl had the impression of watching his reflection in the surface of a rippled pool. Fascinated, he held the image tight in his mind.

Sobel was descending the stairwell from the roof. He reached the fourth floor landing, halted, glanced both ways along the corridor, started down again. He passed the third floor, came to the second. He halted, looked warily around, started along the hall with a slow, stalking tread, one hand jammed into a pocket. He reached the splintered door, paused, listened, glanced around. His hand came out with a blaster. He held it waist-high, stepped quickly into the outer room.

Wehl sensed the consternation in the other's mind as he found it empty. Sobel turned slowly, his eyes drawn to the locked door behind which Wehl waited fearfully. The vision was so strong that Wehl discerned the dark, narrowed eyes, the terrible scar that pulled the mouth awry. His heart began to thud.

He's in there! Sobel's thoughts came with the clarity of speech. The agent reached out, gently tried the knob. Again Wehl sensed the frustration as he found the door locked. Abruptly the barrel of the blaster tilted upward.

"Sobel!" The cry escaped Wehl's lips with sudden fright. "If you blast the door, I'll teleport!" In the silence that followed, he sensed the agent's sudden bewilderment.

Can he? The swift calculation replaced Sobel's confusion.

"You know I can," called Wehl. "You've seen me do it." In the tense, ensuing silence, he had the impression of a dozen plans tumbling through the agent's mind, each discarded as another occurred. Finally a strategem was resolved.

"I want to talk with you," called Sobel.

"You want to kill me!"

"You have a mistaken idea."

"I have? Then why the blaster?" He heard the agent's startled exclamation.

"For my protection," Sobel returned.

"Against whom?"

Sobel struggled with his thoughts. "Hom," he said finally.

"Try again, Sobel."

"He's working on Franckel," the other insisted. "He knows Rayburn's all washed up. He's sold out, Wehl."

"No," Wehl answered softly, "I've read his mind."

"I don't believe that."

"I'm reading your mind, Sobel."

"You can't frighten me with that story, Wehl."

"How did I know who was out there?" Sobel cursed silently. Wehl received the impression of chaotic thoughts. The agent clearly was in a quandary. Wehl found himself enjoying the situation. Then, as the moments passed, the continued silence made him nervous. He had the impression that Sobel had arrived at a plan of action. He tried a shot in the dark. "It won't work," he called.

"What won't?"

"Your plan." He chuckled loudly enough for the agent to hear. Sobel cursed again, then was silent. As the minutes drew out, Wehl realized that time was working against him: Mura and Quigg could be returning very shortly. The possibility was disconcerting. He became aware that the vision of the agent had slipped from his mind and frantically tried to reconstruct it. A blurred image danced in his head, sharpened until the agent's features took form again. His head canted in a listening attitude, Sobel held his ear to the door.

"Trying to locate me?" Wehl called softly.

The agent jerked as if stung. "You're guessing," he charged.

"I'm watching you, Sobel."

"Watching?" The question was tinged with panic.

"I'm clairvoyant."

"You're a liar, Wehl."

"I am?" Wehl chuckled. "You're wearing a brown shirt, tan slacks, a striped summer cape. You're holding the blaster pointed toward the floor."

"Guessing," Sobel called hoarsely.

"No, I see every move you make. I'm reading your

mind, can predict your actions." As he spoke, he became aware of a new presence. Blurry and indistinct, it appeared to split, become multiple. His mind raced, trying to decipher this new phenomenon. He had the impression of movement, whispered voices—three, four, half a dozen men. They seemed floating somewhere above him.

"You'd better come out," Sobel warned.

"Why?"

"You're waiting for the girl, Wehl."

"No," he cried explosively. Panic struck him.

"You sent Quigg to get her." It was Sobel's turn to laugh, a snarling, wolfish laugh. "I maintain a bug on Quigg's communications, Wehl. I listened in."

"You're a liar," he cried. He tried to stifle the turmoil within him.

"How'd you like to see her walk through that door and fry?"

"You wouldn't dare!"

"I wouldn't? Consider my position, Wehl."

"Let me think," he pleaded.

"Take your time, but if the girl gets here first . . ." Sobel laughed nastily. Wehl suppressed the urge to teleport to the other room, try to catch him unaware. Sobel would be waiting for just such a move. But he could teleport into the hall, down to the front entrance . . .

He stiffened involuntarily, caught with the sense of presence again. Please don't let it be Mura, he prayed. He pushed Sobel's image from his mind, tried to locate and identify the newcomer. Again he had the impression of a number of figures; they moved like hazy ghosts in his mind. He sensed they were on the roof.

Abruptly he knew one of the figures was Hom. The knowledge flared in his consciousness with a certainty that staggered him. With a sickening feeling he thought Sobel must have sensed the same thing—the aura of presence was that overpowering.

He flicked his attention back to Sobel. Intent on his quarry, the agent didn't appear aware of anything amiss. How could Sobel not know? A door slammed in the distance and the agent turned, looked toward the hall.

Alarmed, Wehl directed his attention back to Hom. Again the multiple images emerged in his mind, wavering and indistinct. He fought to sharpen his vision. One of the figures solidified, came into focus; he saw it was Hom. The agent was starting down from the roof.

"Careful, careful," Wehl whispered. He was startled to see Hom halt, raise a hand in caution. The agent listened, then moved on again. Awe-struck, Wehl watched him. My God, could he touch Hom's mind, make him understand? The prospect of such a chilling power brought a cold knot to his stomach. That went beyond telepathy—far, far beyond. He shook the feeling aside.

"Hom! Hom! Be careful! Sobel's waiting with a blaster!" He shrieked the warning in his mind. Again the agent stopped in midstride. His head cocked, he gestured the men behind him to remain still. The group froze into a tableau. Reached him, thought Wehl jubilantly.

"Sobel's in the girl's room. He has a blaster." Hom's voice tinkled in Wehl's mind.

"How do you know?" a figure behind the agent whispered.

"I don't know." Hom appeared puzzled. He darted his gaze around with quick, birdlike movements.

A low purring reached Wehl's ears. Aircar! He tore his mind from the agent, filled with the fear that it might be Quigg returning with Mura. Some sixth sense told him the vehicle was landing in front of the building. He heard Sobel's footsteps retreat toward the window.

The sense of a new presence struck him with a blinding force. Two people! Their images danced and flickered in his mind as they emerged from the aircar and entered the building. Man and woman! He felt a frantic dismay.

"Mura! Mura!" He shrieked the name silently, hoping to contact her as he had Hom. When no answering thought came back, he groaned with despair. He'd reached her once—had looked into the long, cool vistas of her mind. Why couldn't he now? But then she'd opened her mind to him, had invited him. He shouted again without effect. Shimmery and indistinct, the figures were like two ghosts at the end of the hall.

Frantically he darted his attention to Hom. Paused on the landing a flight up, the agent was whispering directions to his men. The picture was sharp and clear. *"Hom! Hom! Please hurry,"* he screamed. Hom snapped to rigid attention, gestured quickly and started toward the second floor.

154

"The girl's coming!" Sobel's voice crackled tautly from the other room. "Your last chance, Wehl."

"I'll come out!" He yanked the stun gun from his pocket as he visualized the room in which Sobel stood. The couch, the window, the table with the flowers—its details reeled through his mind. *Sobel stood in a position in which he could cover both doors. Slightly crouched, he held the blaster waist-high. His dark face held a tight, expectant look.*

"No!" The word rocketed and echoed explosively through the corridors of Wehl's mind. He had to stop Sobel! The agent tilted his head, a puzzled expression on his face.

"Drop it, drop it," screamed Wehl.

Sobel stared numbly at the blaster; his hand snapped open and the weapon clattered to the floor.

Wehl teleported.

Instantly, it seemed, he found himself sprawled on the floor next to the couch where he slept. He flipped around to face the agent. Wehl was staring stupidly at the blaster.

"Don't go in there!" Hom's strident warning echoed in the hall. Sobel's head snapped around. He groped wildly for the blaster as a uniformed figure filled the doorway.

"Stop!" Wehl shrieked. Before he could lift the stun gun a dull whoosh filled the room. The figure in the doorway staggered back, head and shoulders outlined in a flickering blue flame.

A woman screamed!

Wehl jerked wildly against the trigger. Sobel's legs buckled. As he fell, the finger on the blaster worked convulsively; a line of fire disintegrated a swath of wall. The window behind Wehl exploded in a clatter of glass.

Wehl fired again. Sobel lurched forward, clawed at the rug; his body jerked spasmodically, then grew still. Wehl struggled to his feet as Hom leaped through the doorway, blaster held low. The agent's eyes took in the scene with a glance. "Thank God," he said. He shoved the blaster inside his jacket.

"Mura?" Wehl croaked.

"She's safe." Hom stepped aside as a woman came through the doorway, her pale face distraught. Madelyn! Wehl stared stupidly at her.

"Father," she exclaimed, "thank heaven you're safe!"

155

Hom inclined his head toward her. "The death of your bodyguard is most regrettable," he murmured. He knelt by Sobel's side, examined him briefly, then ordered his men to carry the unconscious man away.

Madelyn kept her eyes on Wehl. "You have to return before something else happens," she urged. Her voice was edgy.

"I ordered her removed from the ship," said Hom, from the doorway. "She's in safekeeping."

Madelyn eyed him icily.

"Thank you," Wehl told him.

"You'll return?" asked Madelyn.

"Not with you. I'll return with Colonel Hom."

"You'll feel differently when it's over." She fought to conceal her anger. He touched her mind, appalled at the seething hatred he found there, then quickly withdrew. The brief contact had told him all he wanted to know. Madelyn glanced disdainfully at the agent as she left the room.

"She's distraught," Hom murmured apologetically.

"She should be." He smiled faintly. "I promised before to return, but there is a condition."

The agent eyed him gravely. "That is your right," he agreed.

"There will be no succession ceremony."

Hom arched his brows. "Then what's to be gained?"

Wehl told him.

He drifted in darkness. Starless, empty vistas of nothingness stretched into infinity on every side. Where was the sun, the planets, the great sweeping galaxies that gave glory to the sky? Where was time? Had the great clock of the universe run down?

A boy laughed gaily, came running through the darkness. A street formed beneath his feet; the street was peopled. Small shops and apartment dwellings sprang up around him. He ran to the doorway of one of the shops and looked in.

"Hello, Mr. Krant," he called. His voice was piping and young. An old, white-haired man waved from the rear of the shop and the boy raced off again.

A beacon atop a tower swung through the night; aircars darted through it, agleam like small silver moths.

The distorted sky!

A massive planet one by one blotted out the stars . . .

He opened his eyes, stared upward at a white ceiling. For a long moment he held his gaze, his thoughts as nebulous as his dreams. As he shifted his eyes to a tube that ran from one arm to a half-filled bottle of liquid suspended above the edge of the bed his memories seeped back. He rolled his head to one side, grimaced from the sharp pain.

"Easy, easy," a voice cautioned. He caught the shadowy movement as someone came to stand alongside him. Hom! The agent's figure was blurred and indistinct. Wehl tried to focus his eyes.

"I'm back," he said weakly.

"From the dead," Hom agreed. "How do you feel?"

"Shaky." He lifted a hand, gazed at it. Despite the pallor it was large and strong.

"More like your old self?"

"More like my old self," he assented.

"I should apologize," said Hom. "I still don't know how you arrived at the truth."

"The brain transplant?" he considered. "My memories," he said finally.

"Of what?"

"Small things that seeped through the mindblock," he explained. "A candy shop, the tower at the space terminal, the blob that ate the stars—things that couldn't possibly be fitted into Craxton Wehl's life."

"The what?" Hom was startled.

"The blob. That's how I thought of Jupiter as seen from Europa," he explained. "It would be gigantic in the sky. When Mura explained the fish eye, I realized what the blob must be—that the splintered memory of it really was a page from my past. It's the sort of sight we don't see from Earth or Mars, or even from the farther satellites or Jupiter or Saturn. Only Europa really fits the picture. From there was just a step to postulating that I might be Bernard Rayburn."

"Ingenious deduction," Hom murmured appreciatively.

157

"Not really, but if the assumption were true, it struck me that Wehl could be dying because his new body—my body—was rejecting the transplant. Both bodies were; that's what they meant when they told me I was dying."

"You should have been in intelligence."

"Oh, the facts all fitted once I put them together. Wehl's only hope was to regain his old body, give him a chance to try again. That's why I refused to allow the power to be returned. The first succession ceremony was legal; Wehl passed me the power, even though he did steal my body." He chuckled. "So I still have the power."

"I should have guessed earlier," Hom apologized.

"How could you? Have you ever heard of a successful brain transplant before?"

"Never." Hom shook his head. "Wehl was desperate."

"Did he . . . ?"

"He didn't make it the second time," answered Hom softly. "After all, he was seventy-six."

"I'm lucky," he exclaimed.

Hom's lips crinkled. "Sundberg took special pains to make certain you were. It was your life against Pluto."

"Quigg?"

"The worst punishment possible for him. We suspended his charge plate for six months." The agent's voice turned professional. "I also dug out a few other things in the week you've been under."

"The teleportation bit?"

"It wasn't the surgery," Hom affirmed. "You seem to have had quite a record on Europa—the whole gamut of wild talents. Not that I know the full story; those people there are quite close-mouthed."

"I did jump around a bit," he admitted.

Hom scrutinized him questioningly. "I wonder if that's why Wehl selected you—the hope that he might get the power."

"To teleport?" He shook his head. "He couldn't have known. I'm certain the choice was purely political—to stifle the discontent in the OutSats."

"I suppose." Hom smiled again. "Can you remember where you lived as a young boy?"

"Glade Avenue, before my folks went to Europa," he answered promptly. "I can see it in my mind, not as it is but as it was."

158

"Your parents lived in the apartment where Miss Breen now lives," explained Hom.

"So that's why I teleported there!" His eyes caught the agent's. "Mura?" he whispered.

"Feel up to a visitor?"

"Never felt younger," he exclaimed. "Send her in." As the agent left, he sighed happily. It would be great to see Mura again.

It was great to be young.